The Jerry McNeal Series

Rambling Spirit

(A Paranormal Snapshot)

By Sherry A. Burton

The Jerry McNeal Series

Rambling Spirit

By Sherry A. Burton

The Jerry McNeal Series: Rambling Spirit
Copyright 2022

by Sherry A. Burton
Published by Dorry Press
Edited and Formatted by BZHercules.com
Cover by Laura J. Prevost
@laurajprevostphotography

ISBN: 978-1-951386-17-7

For more information on the author and her works, please see www.SherryABurton.com

*To our daughter, Brandy, for overcoming
the odds and giving us a reason to smile.*

To my hubby, thanks for helping me stay in the writing chair.

To my mom, who insisted I keep the dog in the series.

To my editor, Beth, for allowing me to keep my voice.

To Laura, for EVERYTHING you do to keep me current in both my covers and graphics.

To my beta readers for giving the books an early read.

To my proofreader, Latisha Rich, for the extra set of eyes.

To my fans, for the continued support.

Lastly, to my "voices," thank you for all the incredible ideas!

Table of Contents

Chapter One

Jerry stood at the top of the stairs watching as two men loaded his pickup truck onto the back of a flatbed truck. Gunter sat next to him, leaning against his leg as if offering moral support for finally agreeing to let go of the truck his grandmother left him.

It wasn't that he was overly fond of the truck, which took its time starting on occasion, but in the years since he'd owned it, it had never let him down.

Jerry glanced at the new silver Durango Hellcat he'd chosen to take its place, chuckling as he recalled the look on the salesman's face when he'd driven the '73 Ford onto the lot and asked what he could get for a trade. A look significantly trumped when the salesman asked him how long he'd like to finance the loan for, and Jerry told him he intended to pay cash. It wasn't that he was trying to show off – between his inheritance and living a minimalistic lifestyle, he had the money to pay in full. Doing so enabled him to negotiate a significantly reduced sticker price and keep the Ford – opting to donate it to a charity that helped veterans instead.

Gunter gave a low growl. Jerry looked to see the driver headed in his direction. He motioned for Gunter to stay and hurried down the stairs to meet him.

"She's all strapped down. Here's your receipt for the tax write-off." The driver started to leave, then hesitated. "You know you could have gotten a lot more for her if you'd decided to sell her outright."

At least he knew the salesman had been telling the truth. "I know, but it was my granny's truck, and I didn't feel right selling it."

The man wrinkled his brow. "But it felt okay to give it away?"

Jerry shrugged. "I needed something that wouldn't stand out as much."

This comment drew a full-fledged brow raise. "That's your Hellcat, right? You consider it to be less noticeable?"

"I was in a hurry, and it was between that and a minivan. At least with the Durango, I don't have to worry about getting caught." *There's no one chasing you, Jerry. You're the one doing the running.*

The man rocked back on his heels. "Buddy, I don't know what line of work you're in, but if you're hiring, I'm your guy."

There's no correct answer to that, Jerry, so don't even try. "We good here?"

The man sighed his disappointment. "All set."

Jerry waited for him to return to the flatbed before starting up the stairs. As he neared the top of the stairs, Gunter barked, and Jerry looked to see what had gotten the dog's attention. A box truck was at the end of the driveway, waiting to pull in.

Gunter alerted him once more, and Jerry saw his landlord, Todd Wells, standing in the side yard watching the comings and goings while Erma, his Old English Bulldog, balanced precariously on legs much too short to keep her girth from touching the ground.

"What do you think this is, Grand Central Station?" Wells called to him.

Jerry started to give the man the finger, then buried them all into the palm of his hand instead. "You wanted me out. I'm getting out."

The sour expression on Wells' face lifted. "You're leaving today?"

Wells had already pushed him into moving out earlier than the lease called for, though Jerry had every intention of spending the next couple of days in a motel, he decided not to give the man the satisfaction of driving him out even sooner. "You'll get the keys at the end of the month."

The smile disappeared. "If those trucks make ruts in the yard, I'm sending you the bill to have them fixed."

"Don't look now, Wells, but Erma's eating her shit." It was a lie, but Wells jerked the leash so hard, he couldn't have possibly known that the dog was too far away from the pile. Besides, it was rather obvious by looking at the dark mounds around the yard that neither dog nor owner cared enough to clean up the waste.

Jerry looked down and saw Gunter staring back at him with a particularly judgmental expression. "What?"

Gunter yawned and disappeared.

Not for the first time, Jerry envied the dog's ability to disappear at will. "Chicken."

"Excuse me?"

Jerry looked up and saw two men standing just steps away. Both matched him in height. The man who'd spoken held a clipboard and appeared to be at least twenty years his senior. The second man was much younger and seemed on edge as his eyes darted from side to side. If they'd been up to no good, they would've had him at a disadvantage – *Way to go, Marine. Not only did you allow them to get close to you without your knowing it, but here you are talking to yourself.* "I was trying to decide what I wanted for lunch. Come on in."

The man scribbled something on the clipboard he was holding. "What do you have for us?"

Jerry waved a hand around the room, encompassing the couch, a recliner, computer desk, and multiple boxes stacked against the wall. "Take it all. There's a bed and dresser in the bedroom through that door as well. Don't open that door. There's a cat in there that's mad enough by now to scratch your eyes out."

The second man snaked his head around Jerry. "What about the dog?"

Jerry appraised the man for a moment. Unless the dog wanted to be seen, it was rare anyone could see his ghostly K-9 companion. Since the other man hadn't mentioned seeing him, he doubted that to be the case. "My dog's in the bathroom with the cat."

The man tilted his head. "But…"

Jerry cut him off. "It's a large bathroom."

The man with the clipboard walked over to the sofa. "Come on, Jose, we still have two more stops to get in before we can call it a day."

Jose glanced at the bathroom door. "Si, Carlos."

It took eleven trips up and down the stairs to move everything out. Each time Jose returned to the apartment, he looked as if he wanted to question Jerry further about the dog's disappearance. When Carlos came up to have Jerry sign the receipt, he shook his head.

"Jose is new to the job, but I don't think he's going to last long."

"Why is that?"

"He thinks your dog is a *fantasma*."

"Fantasma?"

"Si. He thinks your dog is a ghost."

He is. Jerry forced a smile. "What gave him that

idea?"

"He said you didn't have time to put him in the bathroom, and that if there was a dog, why didn't he bark?"

"That's a good question. One would think if I had a dog in here, he should bark." *Come on, Gunter, take the hint.*

"I told him he was probably a good dog and didn't need to bark."

"Did he believe you?"

"No, and I'm too close to retirement for this. I don't want to work with someone who's loco."

"How about I show him the dog? Would that let him keep his job?"

"He's coming up now. Si, I think that would do it."

Jerry walked to the bathroom door and placed his hand on the handle. "Okay, but if the cat gets out, I can't be held responsible."

Jose entered the room, and Carlos pointed to Jerry. "He wants to show you the dog is real."

Jose's eyes grew wide.

Carlos held up a hand to stop Jerry from opening the door. "Can't you just get him to bark or something?"

Jesus, Jerry, how is this your life? Jerry knocked on the door. "Gunter, I need you to bark." Nothing happened.

Jose whispered something to Carlos.

"Come on, Gunter. There is a lot at stake here." *Like proving I shouldn't be committed and letting this nice man keep his job.* Jerry knocked once more. Relief washed over him when Gunter's bark sounded on the other side of the door. The relief was short-lived when hissing and thuds followed. "Shit! He's trying to kill the cat!"

Jerry reached for the doorknob, intending to defuse the chaos he'd created, and heard another thud – this one coming from the door behind him. When he turned, the two men were gone. Gunter materialized, and they both hurried to the door in time to see both Jose and Carlos running to their collection truck. Jerry looked at Gunter and sighed. "It's a good thing I'm leaving town. My reputation in this one is shot."

Gunter wagged his tail in response.

"You look awfully guilty. Tell me you didn't actually kill the cat."

Gunter licked his lips.

Jerry walked to the bathroom, holding his breath as he opened the door. While the plastic carrier he'd left open was now on its side beside the toilet, Cat was still in one piece and currently sitting on the seabag he'd placed in the shower to keep the collection guys from taking the last of his possessions. Cat growled when Jerry entered, his tail swishing from side to side as his eyes blazed with fear. At that moment, all reservations Jerry had

7

Sherry A. Burton

about his decision to rehome the feline were gone. The dog had made it abundantly clear he was not going anywhere, and as long as Gunter was near, the cat would continue to live in fear.

***

Sergeant Seltzer was at the coffee station when Jerry arrived. The two men locked eyes. His boss finished filling his cup, and Jerry followed him to his office. A lump formed in Jerry's throat as he shut the door and faced the man.

"Why do I have the feeling I'm not going to like what you're getting ready to tell me?"

For a man who claimed to lack intuition, Seltzer always seemed wired into Jerry's feelings. "Because you're probably not."

Seltzer leaned back in his chair and took a sip from his mug.

Just give it to him straight, Jer. "I'm leaving the force."

Seltzer put the cup on his desk and pulled out a pack of gum. He took his time unwrapping two sticks. Jerry knew the man well enough to know he was gathering his thoughts. "I guess I kind of figured this day was coming. We had a good run, you and me."

Seltzer was speaking of the fact that he never treated Jerry like a cop, instead allowing Jerry to act more like a free agent, giving him the freedom to follow his intuition to fight crime. Unlike some, Sergeant Seltzer believed in him and trusted Jerry to act for the greater good of all around him. Jerry smiled. "That we did, sir."

"You good with your decision?"

Not in the least. "Good as I can get."

"You got a plan?"

"Not even an inkling."

"Have a seat, McNeal."

As Jerry sank into the chair, a melancholy crept over him. How many times had he sat across from the man, telling him about a feeling – the two of them bouncing ideas back and forth. Stepping away from the force was one thing, but walking away from a man who'd never once questioned Jerry's authenticity was another. Jerry laced his fingers together to keep them from giving away his anxiety.

Seltzer leaned forward in his chair. "I have faith in you, son. I always have."

Shit. Jerry rolled his neck to ease the tension. "That makes one of us, sir."

Seltzer looked over the desk. "Is your dog going with you?"

"Gunter's not my dog."

Seltzer met his gaze. "The hell he isn't."

"He's here, and so I guess he plans on going."

"Good. I'll sleep better at night knowing someone's got your six."

Jerry ran a hand across the top of his scalp.

"What's troubling you, McNeal?"

Jerry rolled his neck. "What the hell am I doing? For the second time in my life, I'm throwing away a perfectly good career."

"Depends on your definition of 'perfectly good'."

"I'm afraid I'm not following you."

"What's perfectly good for me or, say, Manning in there might not be the same as what's perfectly good for you. Take me, for instance. I'm perfectly fine sitting behind this desk and telling everyone else what to do. Manning is a bit obnoxious, but he's a good police officer. You, on the other hand, have..."

Jerry waited as Sergeant Seltzer searched his mind. *Please don't say spidey senses.*

"You have this gift of knowledge that allows you to know things. That knowledge burdens you with a sense of responsibility to be there when the time comes. Near as I can tell, something like that doesn't fit well in a society with rules and obligations that come with having a real job.

"So how do I make it fit?"

"Damned if I know. You're the one with the spidey senses." Seltzer winked. "Listen, I know you don't like when I call it that, but whether you refer to it as spidey senses, a gift, or a feeling, you were put on this earth with something special. It would be a God-awful shame if you don't get to use it because some of the men in the other room got butthurt because they have to drive a bit further than you on any given day. Take what the man upstairs gave you and do with it what you will. Do it on your own terms and piss on everyone else."

Once Seltzer stepped on his soapbox, he sounded like a Sunday morning preacher. Jerry waited for him to finish his sermon before speaking. "Sir, I sure am going to miss you."

"Miss me? Hell, boy, I'm not going anywhere. I've been saving your sorry ass for six years, and I don't intend to stop now. You find yourself in trouble or just need an ear, I expect you to ring me up on that phone of yours. Understand?"

"Yes, sir, Sergeant!"

Sergeant Seltzer beamed like a proud papa. "Good, now get out there and save the world."

Chapter Two

Jerry glanced in the mirror at the oversized red pickup truck that had been tailgating him for the last eleven miles. Not for the first time, he wished he were driving the old truck his grandmother had left him. If not for the fact his new Durango had less than four hundred miles on it, he would be tempted to slam on the brakes and let the man eat his bumper.

Jerry clamped his hand around the back of his neck, rolling his head from side to side to relieve the tension. In his old life, he would pull the man over. Then again, he doubted the guy would be riding his ass if he knew he was a Pennsylvania State Trooper. Only as of three days ago, he was neither a cop nor a resident of Pennsylvania. *Homeless.*

Jerry laughed. "Don't be so melodramatic, Jerry. You're homeless by choice."

At the sound of his voice, Cat resumed singing the song of a prisoner who'd been tossed into the clink without any hope of parole. Jerry glanced toward Gunter, who sat in the passenger seat beside him. "You were sent here to help, so help. Either beam yourself into that truck behind me and tell that jerk to quit tailgating me or get the cat to be quiet."

Gunter licked his lips in response.

"I don't have a problem with you biting the guy in the truck, but I can't allow you to eat the cat." Why he felt the need to negotiate with the ghost of a K9 police dog, he didn't know.

Gunter yawned.

"Don't give me any of that. If you're bored, go haunt someone else." Jerry checked the mirror once more. "Preferably the man in the truck. Just a quick in and out appearance in the front seat should scare him into backing off."

Jerry turned on his blinker and slid into the passing lane. As happened each time before, the truck followed him into the lane then back into the right lane once more. Jerry wasn't sure if the man was screwing with him on purpose or had simply chosen to follow, hoping to use him as a block against the cops. "I am the cops, dumb shit!" *At least I used to be.*

Gunter turned his head toward the front windshield and barked a single bark.

Jerry looked to see what had gotten the dog's attention. "Not a bad idea." Jerry waited until the last second and took the exit ramp, smiling as the truck continued down the interstate. Jerry slowed to a stop, looked both ways, and took the ramp back to the interstate. Instead of feeling better for ditching the truck, warning bells told him he needed to stop the man. An image of a minivan stopped at the rear of a long line of vehicles waiting to get through construction flashed into his mind. In a rare moment of clarity, Jerry saw the pickup cruise into the back of the same minivan without once tapping the brakes.

Shit.

Jerry's right foot pressed against the gas pedal, a broad smile spreading across his face as the Hemi engine kicked in and he sailed down the onramp, merging back onto Interstate 68. Gliding around a long, winding curve, he pushed the pedal further when the truck came into view, and an image of the carnage soon to occur flashed into his mind.

Gunter barked. Jerry shook off the vision, looked in the side mirror, and saw a state trooper gaining on him. Unless the man was a kindred spirit who'd also picked up on the accident soon to occur, the blue lights were intended for him. The cat wailed its discontent, and Jerry realized it wasn't Cat but the siren from the police car. He knew better than to keep going, but while stopping would keep him out of trouble, doing so would be fatal to the family of five the man in the pickup was going to encounter in the next couple of miles.

Seltzer. Jerry pushed the button on the steering wheel to bring the Uconnect to life. "Call Seltzer."

"McNeal? Tell me this means you've reconsidered your resignation."

Jerry didn't have time for pleasantries. "I need that life ring you offered."

Seltzer laughed a nervous laugh. "Jesus, McNeal, what's it been? Seventy-two hours? Are those sirens I hear?"

"Long story. Listen, I'm in West Virginia, Interstate 68, just before Morgantown. I've got a trooper on my ass and can't stop."

"West Virginia? What do you mean you can't stop? Are your brakes out?"

"Come on, Seltzer, I don't have time to play Twenty Questions. Just make the call. I doubt they have more than one police chase going on around here. Tell them I'll stop as soon as I get the truck pulled over." Jerry switched off the phone and crossed into the left lane. Pulling alongside the truck, he honked the horn to get the driver's attention. It took nearly a full minute for the man to look in his direction. When he did, Jerry jerked a thumb behind him and motioned the man to pull over.

The guy looked in his mirror and immediately slowed, moving to the emergency lane. In that instant, the feeling of doom that surrounded the man lessened, leaving a small mountain of worry in its path. Knowing the trooper would not put himself in harm's way by pulling in front of him, Jerry maneuvered his SUV in front of the pickup truck so he wouldn't be able to pull out without backing up.

Jerry breathed easier when the trooper followed protocol and pulled in behind the truck. *Calm down, Jerry; you did what you needed to do.*

Jerry pulled out his wallet and temporary registration, placing them in his lap, then rolled down his windows before placing both hands on the wheel.

While Gunter made himself scarce, Cat revved up the volume, meowing his discontent.

The trooper made no move to get out of his cruiser, and Jerry knew he was waiting for backup. All for the best. It would give Seltzer more time to contact them and smooth things over. An image of Seltzer leaning back in his chair, chewing on a stick of gum and trying to explain why he'd known to call came to mind. *Shit, Jerry, you're causing more problems for the man now than you ever did when you worked for him. How's it going to sound when he tells them you get feelings and they should just let you go?* "Quiet, Cat."

Two additional units – one carrying two officers – pulled up. Jerry watched as the team cleared the pickup truck – one taking the man back to a waiting cruiser. Once they had the truck secured, the three remaining officers proceeded toward Jerry, approaching on each side of his vehicle. One positioned himself at the right rear of the Durango; the original trooper kept his hand on the handle of his pistol as he and the other officer stopped just behind the left passenger door.

"Don't look now, boys, but I think I'm about to be arrested." The words had no sooner left his mouth than Gunter disappeared. *So much for having my back.*

The officer to the right moved forward, checking the cargo space before signaling for the original trooper to proceed.

The trooper searched the inside of the front cabin with his eyes. "License and registration."

"I need to lower my hands."

"Any weapons in the vehicle?"

Jerry kept his hands in place, knowing his personal arsenal lay tucked beneath the seats. "Yes, sir." *Please don't ask how many.*

"How about I just have you step out of the vehicle."

Shit! Don't let them put you in handcuffs. Handcuffs mean jail. Keep them talking; give Seltzer time to work his magic. "I'm going to take my hands off the wheel to open my door."

The officer nodded then stepped back to give him room. "Move around to the front of the vehicle."

Jerry did as told.

"Care to tell me why you took so long to stop?"

Jerry pointed to his SUV where the cat's angry cries filled the air and shrugged. "Didn't hear you."

"I guess you didn't see my lights either."

"The sun was in my eyes." *How many times had*

he heard that one?

The officer glanced at the Durango. "Do you give us permission to search the vehicle?"

Jerry took in a deep breath, wondering how many guns his weapons permit covered. *He has probable cause. Admit it, Jerry; you've used it with less evidence.* He shook his head. "No."

"We can get a warrant."

You can, but it will take some time. Come on, Seltzer, make the call. Jerry sighed and leaned against the front of his Durango. "Listen, you've got me on speeding, but that's it. I admitted to having a weapon, which I have a permit to carry. That doesn't give you the right to search my vehicle."

"You were speeding down the onramp, took your time stopping, and when you did, you involved another vehicle. It's enough."

"The guy was tailgating me. I decided to give him some room, so I took the off-ramp. I looked at him as he passed, intending to give him the bird, and thought I saw him nodding off behind the wheel. Instead of letting him kill someone, I thought I'd try to stop him." Okay, it was mostly true – he'd only left off the most crucial part. *Better to have them think you're a nut job than to have them sifting through the burned remains of a minivan with a family inside.*

"And you want to make a citizen's arrest?"

Something like that. Before Jerry could drum up

an answer, a second officer joined them.

"Here's your license and registration, Trooper McNeal."

Trooper?

"You mean you're on the job?"

Not anymore.

The officer handed Jerry his license and registration then looked at the West Virginia State Trooper. "McNeal here is one of you, out of Pennsylvania."

The trooper didn't seem amused. "You didn't feel the need to share that with me when I asked if you have any weapons?"

The officer laughed. "He was probably too embarrassed. According to the database, McNeal lost his ID and badge and is waiting for a replacement."

He had to give it to Seltzer; the man was creative.

The fourth officer joined them. "Everything under control?"

"Yeah. What's the deal with your guy? Our friend here thought he was nodding off at the wheel."

"Could have been. He said he hasn't slept much in the last couple of days – broke up with his girlfriend and is pretty upset. It's probably a good thing he got stopped, as it gave him a chance to get his head together. He's on his way to her place now to pick up his belongings. It's in county, so I'm going to follow him to make sure there aren't any problems."

The trooper gave a nod to Jerry. "You're free to go, but a word of advice: next time, suck up the embarrassment and save everyone a lot of trouble. Miller, hold up, I'll follow you, and we'll grab some grub afterward."

The other two officers smiled then followed at a slower pace. Jerry instantly felt the remaining anxiety lift. Most of it anyway, as he still had another four hundred miles to go with the cat, who continued to wail the blues from inside the Durango. *Five and a half hours. Maybe I should have let them arrest me. At least then I'd have gotten a few hours of peace.*

Jerry rolled up the windows and dialed Seltzer's number, pulling back onto the freeway as he waited for the man to pick up.

"It's too early for your one phone call, so I take it my little ruse worked?"

"If you mean did they think me an oaf for losing my badge and ID and let me go out of pity, then yes."

"Is that sirens?"

"No, it's my damn cat."

Seltzer chuckled. "Remind me never to ride with you."

"So why not tell them a story and get me off on a professional courtesy?"

"I got to thinking about it after you left the other

day. I thought this might be a better solution in case I am not reachable when you need me. This way, they run your record, and it will show up in the database."

"How long do you think we'll be able to get away with this charade?"

"Hell if I know. I'll keep an eye on things on my end until you figure out your next move."

"And if I don't?"

"You will. But as long as you're not drawing a paycheck, there shouldn't be any reason for anyone in this department to pull your record."

"You're going out on a big limb, Sergeant."

"Did you save the day, McNeal?"

A feeling of absolute certainty washed over him. "Just up the road, there is a family – mother, father, and three children, one of them only a few weeks old – who will now make it to their destination."

"And if you hadn't intervened?"

Jerry shivered. "Not good, sir, not good at all."

"That's all I need to hear. You be careful out there, McNeal. There's a lot of good people depending on you."

"But no pressure."

"Only the pressure you put on yourself."

Chapter Three

Jerry pulled into the driveway, admiring not only the old farmhouse but the land it was sitting on. A line of trees hedged the northwest side of the property; a large barn sat just to the east of the house. Several horses grazed in the field. One looked up and tossed its head, questioning the new arrival. An image of a winged horse flashed in his mind. Jerry did a double-take, needing to ensure they were, in fact, just horses.

A large, fluffy white dog stood just outside his driver's side door, alerting the residents to his arrival. The dog's tail was wagging, and Jerry wished Gunter would return to ensure his safety. Jerry honked the horn, expecting Savannah to call the dog off. When she didn't, he opened the door and stuck out his left foot. When the dog sniffed his boot but didn't attack, the rest of him followed, pulling the cat carrier from his SUV as Cat grumbled his displeasure. Holding the carrier well out of reach of the dog, Jerry shut the door and made his way to the house, pressing his index finger against the doorbell. While he waited, he brought the carrier up so he could see the angry feline. Cat hissed and clawed at the metal grate. Jerry looked at the dog and thought about opening the plastic box. *Sorry, dog. My money's on the cat this time.*

"Not to worry, Cat, you're going to like it so much better here. Lots of land to explore and not a ghost dog in sight." The last part bothered him, as he hadn't seen any sign of Gunter since his run-in with the law in West Virginia.

The door opened. Savannah took one look at Jerry and shook her head. "Don't you look like the sorry soul!"

Wearing grey sweats with her dark hair pulled into a ponytail, she looked like the girl next door. Not the sultry, bosom-flaunting psychic medium she portrayed when giving readings. Jerry handed her the container. "Here's your beast. You're both lucky he's not in a shelter in Maryland right now."

Savannah looked in the carrier and made kissy sounds at the cat. "Long trip?"

"Made even longer by a cat that wouldn't shut up and tried to claw me to death every time I got near the carrier."

"I offered to bring him with me when I left, but you told me no."

"A decision I may regret for the rest of my life."

Savannah peeked in the carrier once more. "It's okay, big guy. I'll save you from that bad man."

"Bad enough to give him a home and feed him

so he didn't have to stay outside and freeze to death."

She lowered the carrier. "I guess you're not such a bad guy after all. Care to come in?"

Jerry looked past her. "Your wife won't mind?"

Savannah raised an eyebrow. "I asked you to come into my house, not share my bed."

"Too bad. I could use a nap about now."

Savannah moved away from the door. "Kick your boots off and come into the kitchen. Let me show him where the litterbox is, and I'll make you a cup of coffee. Don't let the dog in – he's a working dog. It's his job to protect the livestock."

Jerry placed his boots on the rug and stood, arching his back for a moment before making his way into the kitchen. "Don't go putting yourself out. You don't have to make a pot on my account."

Savannah laughed an easy laugh and pointed to the pod machine on the counter. "I can bake anything you want, but that there's the extent of my coffee knowledge."

"The shifts I work call for a great deal of caffeine." Jerry sighed a heavy sigh. "Used to work, that is."

"I have to admit I was surprised when you called and said you'd actually done it."

"Not any more surprised than my sergeant when I told him I was resigning."

"Was he mad?"

"Seltzer, nah. I'd like to think I surprised him, but a bigger part of him expected it."

Savannah grew quiet for a moment, and he knew she was reading him. She tilted her head. "Why do I get the feeling you still work for him?"

"I think 'work' is too much of a stretch."

"Maybe. But the two of you are still connected?"

"He knows all my dark secrets."

"Lucky him." She winked. "Why does he come across as a father figure?"

Jerry raised an eyebrow. "Seltzer is the kind of person that's easy to talk to. He listens without judging and I guess you could say he believes in me. Unlike my real father, who has never understood me. Seltzer offered to help out if I find myself in a jam."

"Like the one earlier today? Were you really in a police chase?"

He was glad she was married; a relationship with her wouldn't stand a chance. "Do I need to tell you about it, or can you just beam the information from my mind?"

This elicited a giggle. "I'm not that good."

"If I'm going to tell it, I'm going to need that coffee."

A blush crept over her face, and she pulled a cup from the cabinet and set it under the machine. As she fiddled with the pod, Jerry began to speak. "I had a truck tailgating me. The dog suggested I give him some space, so I took the off-ramp."

She turned toward him, her eyes wide. "The dog's talking to you now?"

Jerry smiled and shook his head. "Not in the sense you're thinking, but he barked, and I knew what he wanted me to do."

"Jerry, that is amazing."

"It is?"

"Sure it is. When I talk to the animals, I don't talk to them like you and I are talking right now. I can just… I don't know, hear them in my mind."

Jerry scratched his head. "I might need some bourbon in that coffee."

"I'm sorry, go on with your story."

"The moment the truck passed, I knew it was a mistake – that I was the only thing between him and something horrific. I tried to catch him and had the whole West Virginia police force on my ass." He'd purposely left out some things and exaggerated others to see how she responded.

She looked him up and down. "Something's changed."

"You mean besides the fact that the cat isn't meowing?"

She handed him the steaming cup of coffee and joined him at the table. "You like it black, right?"

"Yes."

"He's happy to be out of the carrier. That's not what I was talking about. I meant this vision was different."

He nodded.

"Tell me about it."

Though he'd spent the last four hundred miles dissecting it, he still wasn't sure where to start. "As long as I can remember, the feeling always begins with a tingling. A neck crawl or the simple knowledge that something is going to happen."

"And today?"

"It was instantaneous. I knew who, what, and when." He took a sip of the coffee. "I saw it."

"Like a picture or a movie?"

"Both, I guess. First, it came across like a snapshot, and then it was as if a movie was playing in my head. Only I didn't have to concentrate. It was just there."

"Your eyes were open?"

"I sure hope so. I was blasting down the interstate at the time."

"And it's never happened before?"

"Not like that...nothing like that, ever."

"Where was the dog?"

"In the seat beside me."

"And now?"

"Don't know. He disappeared when the police showed up, and I haven't seen him since. I figured he got tired of listening to the cat's bellowing. God knows I did. You don't think he's gone gone, do you?"

She shook her head. "Doubtful. I just wonder if your powers are growing because of the dog."

He looked over the cup at her. "My powers? Now you sound like Sergeant Seltzer. I'm not a superhero and I don't have any powers."

"Would you prefer me to call them your gifts?"

"I've always called them my feelings."

She raised an eyebrow. "Jerry, you and I both know they are more than that."

"Well, I feel things…or at least I used to. Now I see things, unless it was just a one-time thing. Do you think it will happen again? Maybe it was just because I didn't have time to let things play out."

"Why not?"

"For one thing, the police were chasing me, and for another, if I would have let things play out, people would have gotten killed. A whole family. One of them not even old enough to have had a bad dream."

"The timing could've had something to do with it for sure. But I think there's more to it. I think it is because you've finally found your path."

He set down his empty cup and stared at her. "What path? I'm thirty-two years old, unemployed, and currently living out of my vehicle. You may think this is freedom, but frankly, it scares the hell out of me."

If she could tell he was on the verge of a panic attack, it didn't show. She simply licked her lips and continued as if everything was right with the world. Her world maybe, but not his – his was hanging on by a kite string. The cat jumped into her lap, and for a moment, he felt a twinge of jealousy. She lifted her eyes and gave him an incredulous look. "You can't have it both ways."

"I don't know what you're talking about."

"That's a crock. You don't like the cat. How do you expect him to like you?"

"I like him a little."

She rubbed at the side of the cat's face, and Cat purred, pressing into her hand. "You're welcome to take him with you."

Not a chance. "He seems content to stay with you."

"Okay, have it your way, but once you walk out that door, the offer's off the table."

"Promise?"

"You seem calmer now."

He thought she was talking to Cat for a moment, then realized she'd aimed her comment at him. "Maybe. I guess I'm just trying to figure out the age-old question."

"Which is?"

"What am I going to be when I grow up?"

"Who says you have to grow up?"

He laughed. "My father."

"He doesn't have the gift, does he?"

"No. Neither does my mother."

"And yet she understands it."

"Her mother – my grandmother – had it. I guess it's easier to understand when you're raised around it."

"Something tells me that's where you need to start. Yes, yes, I'm sure of it, something to do with family. Something from the past that you need to revisit will help you get closure so you can move forward. Does that make sense?"

More than you know. "I don't think that would be a good idea."

"You haven't told your family that you quit the force?"

"No, and I don't intend to either."

"You don't do well with lies, Jerry."

"That's why I'm not going home."

"Where is home?"

"Parked in your driveway. Everything I own is stuffed inside a seabag in the back seat. Everything else I either donated or gave away. I told you it's a sorry life."

She ignored his attempt to bring her into his pity party. "Where do your parents live?"

"Florida."

"No, that's not right."

He raised an eyebrow. "That's where I send their Christmas card."

"Then why am I seeing mountains?"

Shit. Because someone decided the annual family

reunion should be held at Uncle Marvin's house this year. He had had excuses as to why he couldn't attend in the past. As of three days ago, he was a free agent. If anyone in the family found out he was unemployed, he would have no choice but to go – *and tell them what? That he'd quit his job again.* Jerry felt his jaw tense. "I'm not going."

Savannah raised an eyebrow. "I hate to say it, but your grandmother just showed up. She said you're supposed to be nice to the guy."

Jerry knew she was near; he could feel her presence. "If she's here, why is the cat not reacting?"

Savannah shrugged. "My guess is because it's not a malicious spirit."

"That's kind of what I've gotten before. That doesn't explain why I can't hear or see her."

"I don't know. But she's saying you have to go to the family reunion. Something about looking out for Marvin."

"Marvin can go to … I could give a care less what happens to my uncle."

"She's repeating herself. Saying you need to go and that she knows you feel it."

Jerry fought the anger that threatened to sour his previously good mood. He did feel the pull – that was the problem.

"She told me to remind you that Marvin didn't have anything to do with Joseph's death. And that you holding it against him isn't helping anyone. Tell me about Joseph's death."

Jerry pushed from his chair. "Listen, I appreciate your taking Cat off my hands. And I know that you're only trying to help, but I came here to drop off a cat, not have a therapy session."

Savannah stood and moved to the counter. "I'm sorry, I sometimes forget myself – especially when things come through this strong. Your grandmother – no, she's telling me to call her Granny. Granny wants me to tell you she's sorry too but says it's important that you go."

"Why am I here?"

"You dropped off a cat, remember?"

Jerry laughed. "My ears are still ringing from listening to his constant meowing. But that's the point – he wasn't even my cat. Not really; he just showed up at my door one day."

"Did you try to find his owner?"

"Of course. I called the vets in the area and put up signs. Hell, I even paid for an ad in the paper."

"I hate to be the bearer of bad news, but if you did all that and didn't take him to the SPCA, he's your cat."

"Let's say for the sake of argument he was my cat. I could have simply opened the door and let him outside. Or, I could have found him a home in Pennsylvania. Why Louisville, Kentucky? Why you?"

"Because I was convenient?"

"Spending eternity locked up inside a vehicle with that cat is not what I'd call convenient." He ran a hand over his head, momentarily surprised to feel stubble, then remembered he'd stopped shaving his scalp two days prior. *Three days off the job, and I've already turned into a wild man.* Jerry shook off the thought.

"Why West Virginia?"

"Excuse me?"

"You could have come through Ohio. Why did you decide to go through West Virginia?"

Jerry looked at the cat, who was investigating every inch of the kitchen. "Glutton for punishment?"

"Or maybe you were guided there. If not for you, that family would have died."

A chill ran down Jerry's spine. "So, what? I'm just to drive around the country and wait for something to happen that I'm supposed to try to fix?"

"It worked for Michael Landon on *Highway to Heaven.*"

Jerry closed his eyes then opened them once more. "I'm not an angel."

"Neither was Michael's friend, but you both travel with one."

This evoked a laugh from Jerry. "You've met the dog, right? He's no angel."

"The two of you just have to work on your trust issues."

Jerry lifted his cup from the table and placed it into the sink. "You're in the wrong line of work. You really need to become a therapist."

"Then allow me to give you this bit of advice. You're looking for answers, Jerry. Maybe you should listen to your grandmother's advice and go to the reunion. It seems pretty important to her."

Jerry looked at the orange cat who'd made himself at home and was currently lounging on the counter, purring his contentment as Savannah ran a hand down the length of him. *I think I'll come back as a cat in my next life.* "Cat knows he's not allowed on the counter."

"My house, my rules. Isn't that right, Gus?"

Jerry lifted an eyebrow. "Gus?"

She winked. "It's a lot better than Cat."

"We'll agree to disagree on that." Jerry paced the length of the kitchen then walked to the refrigerator staring at the photos. He keyed on one of Savannah standing next to a woman in a police uniform. The instant he saw the picture, the hair on the back of his neck prickled.

Savannah moved up beside him. "My wife."

"You didn't tell me she's on the job."

"You didn't ask."

Chapter Four

Jerry scanned the photos and selected the one that spoke the clearest. Both Savannah and her wife, Alex, wore simple, long, light purple dresses, and each had their hair pulled away from their face. Each had an arm draped around the other's back, and their facial expressions exuded happiness. He turned, holding the photo for her to see. "Your wedding photo?"

"Yes. Some of our family didn't approve, so it was just a simple ceremony with a few friends and what family chose to attend."

"Your family doesn't like Alex?"

"The problem isn't Alex. She's great. Just ask anyone." Savannah blew out a sigh. "It's that I chose to marry her they have an issue with. You'd think Cassidy would be more open, but my sister is the worst of the bunch."

"Give them time, they'll come around." Jerry wanted to laugh. He was the last one qualified to give family advice.

Savannah shrugged off his comment. "Don't make no difference to me."

35

It was a lie, and he knew it. "You two didn't happen to honeymoon in Hawaii, did you?"

"I wish. No, we spent a few days in Myrtle Beach."

Shit. He really wished she would have said yes. "And Alex doesn't have any family there?" He knew the answer but had to ask.

"No." Savannah took the picture from him and studied it. "There is nothing in the picture that even looks like Hawaii. Why all the questions?"

Jerry scratched the back of his scalp. "Just a feeling."

Savannah raised an eyebrow. "That we are going to Hawaii?"

"No."

Savannah held the picture with both hands. "You think Alex is going to Hawaii without me?"

"No. I think Hawaii is coming here."

"Tell me that's a good thing." He hesitated, and she narrowed her eyes. "Dammit, Jerry, Answer me."

He walked to the table, hoping Savannah would follow. When he turned to look at her, she was shaking. *Easy, Jerry.* "It's too early to tell."

"What do you mean too early? You said you got the information instantly today! What are you not telling me, and why the hell can't I feel it?"

He understood her frustration. He'd been feeling the same thing for years. Getting a feeling and not having enough information to stop it in advance or knowing something was going to happen and staying patient enough not to alter the course. "I don't know. Maybe for the same reason I can't see Granny. Maybe you are too close."

"That's not good enough. You have to know! This is Alex." She closed her eyes, blinking away tears. "This is MY life!"

Jerry waited for her tears to subside before speaking. "I can't give you answers I don't have. All I know... well, I don't know it, but it makes sense. Maybe that's why I'm here – to try to stop whatever it is."

"Try?"

Be honest, Jerry. "I can't always stop it."

"Is she going to die?" Her words came out as a sob.

"Not if I can help it." He raised a hand to silence her. "Whatever it is could be serious. Why else bring me here? With that said, you didn't tell me Alex is a cop, so maybe I just needed to come here so that I could see the picture."

She joined him at the table. "Do you think that's the case?"

"I think it's too early to tell. Maybe that's why it came to me in a movie earlier because it was going to happen soon. Right now, I'm only getting snippets. Snapshots, if you will."

Cat climbed onto Savannah's lap, and she sat

absently stroking him. *How many times did he try that with you, Jerry, and you pushed him away? Where's the dog? What's the matter, Jerry? Feeling left out? This is not a popularity contest. Stay on point.* Jerry rolled his neck to get out of his head. "Listen, just because I know something's going to happen doesn't mean things aren't going to work out. Look at what happened with you in Pennsylvania. That turned out alright."

"I just don't understand why I didn't pick up on it." She closed her eyes briefly then opened them once again. "I still don't feel anything."

"I'm not lying."

"I wish you were."

"Me too."

She brushed away a tear. "Now what?"

"We wait."

Savannah pushed off from her chair and placed the cat on the floor. She went to the drawer and pulled out a writing tablet and some pencils, placing them on the table in front of him.

"What are these for?"

"I need to see what you see."

"You expect me to draw what's in my head?"

"Yes, unless your brain is hooked into a printer."

"Not the last time I checked."

"Then draw what you see."

Jerry resisted rolling his eyes. "You know I usually work alone, right?"

"Yep, but that is all behind you. You have me and the dog now."

"I've not seen the dog since I left West Virginia, and when did you get added into the equation?"

"When you set your sights on my wife." She winked and handed him a pencil.

Jerry placed the lead on the paper and drew a circle and several lines. When he finished drawing the stick figure, he turned the paper for her to see.

Savannah sighed. "Really, Jerry?"

"It's Alex. Don't you see the resemblance?"

"I think she needs to eat a sandwich. Seriously, is this the best you can do?"

"When I say it's early, I'm serious. I can see Alex, and I can feel Hawaii."

"Because it feels warm?"

Jerry rubbed at his temples. "This is why I work alone. I should probably go give the image time to grow."

"Go? You're leaving town?" Savannah's eyes were round, reminding him of a deer caught in the headlights. "What about Alex?"

"I never said I was leaving town. I'm going to find a hotel and take a shower."

"You can stay here. We have three guest rooms."

"I appreciate the offer, but I need to clear my mind. I promise to call if I get anything else."

"What do I tell Alex?"

He turned to face her, keeping his emotions in

check. "Nothing."

"I can't do that. Alex will be able to read my face."

"Alex is psychic?"

"No. But she knows me well enough to know when something's wrong."

"Tell her you took a nap and had a dream about what went on in Pennsylvania. She knows how upset you were, so that should pass the sniff test."

"Why not tell her the truth?"

"We don't know what the truth is. Right now, all we know is I see Alex in some kind of trouble."

"Exactly. So we should tell her."

"Telling her could put her in even more danger. Alex is a cop and, as such, has to make split-second decisions every day of her life. What if she starts second-guessing herself or hesitates at the wrong time? It's best for her if we keep this to ourselves for now. We alter her routine, and we could alter whatever I'm feeling. That happens, and I might not be able to do anything. Let me do what I do. I might not be good at much, but this I can do. This works whether I want it to or not. It is already pinging on Alex – let's let it do what it does."

Savannah nodded her head. "Okay, Jerry. We'll do it your way. I promise not to tell Alex."

Jerry started for the door. "I'm going to drive around for a bit and see if I can pick up anything."

"Haven't you had enough driving for one day?"

"It will be nice to have some peace and quiet. Tuck your lip back in; I was talking about the cat."

"He didn't mean that, Gus."

Jerry looked at the orange cat, who didn't seem the least bit upset over his leaving. "Oh, I assure you, I did."

"Jerry, hang on a second." Savannah ran down the hall and returned a moment later, handing him a small picture frame along with a bracelet. "It's a picture of Alex and her favorite bracelet."

"I know what she looks like."

"I know, but I find I can get a better reading if I hold something personal. Louisville is a lot bigger than Chambersburg and has a lot more people, especially with all the Derby festivities. People will be coming in from all over. I wouldn't want you to start following any false leads."

Best to humor her, or you'll never get out of here. "It's probably not a bad idea. Derby festivities?"

"Yes, the Kentucky Derby. It's a horse race. Surely you've heard of it?"

"Yes, I've heard of the Kentucky Derby. But you said Derby festivities."

"Used to only be the race, but now they have all kinds of activities leading up to the race."

"Like what?"

"Thunder over Louisville, Chow Wagons, steamboat races, a parade, Barnstable Brown party.

They have the balloon glow and the great balloon race. Oh, and the Oaks race is Friday, but there is another race Thursday night. It started as something for the locals who didn't want to fight the crowds on Derby Day, but it has gotten so big, they named it. Thurby – Thursday and Derby. People dress up, and really it's just a mini-version of the Derby."

Everything pinged, and yet nothing told him that was what he was looking for. "This might sound crazy."

She laughed. "In my line of work, nothing sounds crazy."

"Does a winged horse mean anything?"

Savannah blinked. "You're kidding, right?"

"Not usually."

"Jerry, everything this week has to do with winged horses. Tours, parties. They use the Pegasus pins as admission to some of the big events. Heck, even the parade is called the Pegasus Parade. Jerry, please tell me that's not all you have to go on."

Shit. "It's not, but when I saw your horses, I saw a horse with wings. I figured I'd been on the road too long."

"But we both know there's more to it than that, don't we?"

Jerry placed a hand on her shoulder. "It's early. Don't go getting yourself all worked up. I will call you in the morning, and remember, not a word to Alex."

She nodded, and he knew there would be tears the moment he was gone. He could say something now and open the waterfall, but he didn't do well with tears, so he turned and walked out the door without another word.

***

Once inside the Durango, Jerry placed the photo and bracelet in the center console, leaned his head against the headrest, and closed his eyes. Savannah said there were a lot of festivities, which meant lots of crowds and parties. *Way to go, Jerry. Why'd you even let on there was a problem? Not only did you tell her of imminent doom, but you also led her to believe you're Nicholas Cage here to save the freaking day. And why not bring Alex in on things? She's a patrol cop in a vast city. How do you expect to find her without help?*

Jerry put his palms together in prayer form. *Think, Jerry.* The feeling around Alex definitely came across as Hawaii – *maybe a luau? So, what do you search the internet for Louisville or luau? Or, you just let the feeling guide you. Come on, Jerry, this is what you do, so why all of the sudden are you second-guessing your abilities? Because I've let myself get too involved.* Jerry remembered Manning's accusation – you help everyone but those you care about.

Jerry opened his eyes and plucked the bracelet from the console, gripping it in his hand as he'd seen Savannah do with his watch when she'd given him his reading. An image of a rainbow came to mind. *No real surprise there; Alex is gay.* Jerry set the bracelet aside and picked up the photo of Alex in a standard-issue police uniform, staring back at him as if to say *Well, are you going to help me or not?* Jerry started to feel a stab of panic setting in. *Easy, Jerry. You don't have time for this.*

He placed the photo in the console, took his cell phone out of his pocket, scrolled through his preprogrammed numbers, and dialed.

"Talk to me, Jerry?" At the sound of Doc's voice, the panic ebbed.

"I quit the force."

"How's that working out for you?" That was what Jerry liked about his conversations with Doc. The man had heard it all and withheld judgment, at least while on the phone.

"Still trying to figure things out."

"You will."

"Do you really think so?"

"McNeal, if there is one person I don't worry about, it's you. That gift of yours is like a built-in radar. Follow the beacon, and it will lead you to where you're supposed to go."

Good ole Doc, always saying the right thing.

Jerry instantly felt as if a weight lifted from his

shoulders. "Got to go, Doc."

"You good, Jerry?"

Jerry nodded his reply. "Thanks, Doc."

Laughter floated through the phone. "Was that gratitude I just heard?"

"There's a first for everything."

"I'll drink to that."

The hairs on the back of Jerry's neck prickled. "You good, Doc?"

"Golden."

"You need anything, you have my number."

Another laugh. "Go save the world, McNeal."

Another prickle. It was the same phrase Seltzer had used. Jerry ended the call and pocketed his phone. *I'll settle for saving a five-foot-nine police officer with hazel eyes.*

Chapter Five

Jerry leaned his head against the headrest and closed his eyes. If not for the tug from his intuition, he would have no trouble putting his seat back and taking a nap. He felt himself falling and jerked his head to prevent it. Opening his eyes, he saw Gunter staring at him. Jerry smiled.

"Welcome back."

Gunter woofed his reply.

"I thought maybe you'd decided to stay with one of the officers in West Virginia."

Gunter growled a low growl.

"It looks like we're staying in the area for a bit. I got a hit on something. I'm not sure how big just yet, but I think it's the reason I'm here."

Gunter growled once more, this one deeper than the first.

"Oh, my bad, the reason we're here."

Gunter gave a yipped response.

"The thing is, I'm a bit nervous about this one."

Gunter tilted his head.

"Yeah, I think I'm too close. I like Savannah."

Gunter's lip curled and he emitted a slight growl.

Jerry suddenly felt as if the dog were scolding him for trying to steal someone's girl. "I know she's married. She's a friend, and therein the problem. I don't want to screw this up. What if I can't figure it out? What if I can't save the day?"

Gunter surprised Jerry by placing his paw on top of Jerry's hand. It was a small gesture, but Jerry felt it just as much as if the dog would have verbally told him to quit worrying. *We will figure this out together*. And at that moment, Jerry knew it to be true.

Jerry spent the next couple of hours driving. He took Interstate 65 through downtown Louisville and continued across the bridge to Indiana, taking the first exit then retracing his path. Traffic was thick – at times, Jerry found himself creeping along at a crawl. Even with Gunter's help, navigating the crush of traffic worried him. Without a siren, he would have no option but to move along at a snail's pace. That scenario did not bode well if his feelings intensified. Jerry looked at Gunter. "Any ideas on how in the hell we're going to make this work?"

Gunter lowered his head and came up holding the end of the photograph in his teeth. Jerry took it from him. *Come on, Jerry, you're not going to get any answers like this.*

Jerry saw a sign for a motel and took the exit. As he pulled up to the front of the building, Gunter groaned.

"You don't approve?" When the dog didn't respond, Jerry went inside.

The lobby was packed full of people waiting to check in. Jerry bided his time until, at last, he was standing at the counter across from a woman whose name tag read "Bev."

Bev had bags under her eyes and looked as if she could use a room of her own. She looked up from the computer screen. Nearly double his age, a pink blush crept over her cheeks as she eyed him up and down. "Checking in?"

"Yes, I'd like a room for the week."

The color faded as she raised an eyebrow. "You don't have reservations?"

"No."

"Honey, I'm sorry. We're full."

Jerry ran a hand over his scalp. "Can you recommend another hotel?"

Bev shook her head. "Derby is our biggest tourist event. The city gets over seven hundred thousand visitors this month. Why, I doubt you're going to find a hotel, bed and breakfast, or air B&B within a hundred-mile radius of the city."

"That explains all the traffic."

"Honey, this is Louisville; there's always traffic." The lobby doors opened. Jerry followed the woman's gaze and saw a middle-aged man wheeling a suitcase. The second Jerry saw him, the hairs on the back of his neck started to prickle. Bev sighed and handed Jerry a brochure that listed the Derby festivities. Their hands touched – instantly, Jerry saw her fighting for her life in the parking lot outside the hotel. As the image progressed, he realized she was lying in a pool of blood, and he knew she had been stabbed. *Shit!*

Jerry pretended to yawn. "I've been on the road all day. Would you have a problem with me taking a nap in my vehicle to take the edge off?"

Bev smiled a sympathetic smile. "No, Sugar, you go right ahead. My car – a white Ford Focus – is parked on the west side of the building. No one likes to park over there because the light is out. I've called, but they're taking their time coming to fix it. Park over there. It'll be darker and quieter for you. There's a bathroom in the lobby if you need it."

Jerry turned and purposely brushed against the arm of the man behind him. Instantly, an image of him changing a tire on the side of the interstate flashed before his eyes. Jerry looked the man in the eye and saw another flash. This time, the guy was clipped by a passing vehicle as he attempted to get back into his car. A third flash saw him being dragged by the vehicle that had sideswiped him. Jerry mumbled his apologies and hurried toward the door. Once outside, he stood processing everything he'd just seen. On the surface, both images appeared to be connected, but as he rolled the images over in his head, he knew he'd just come face-to-face with two unlucky individuals. In a city this large, it was doubtful he would be able to get through the day without pinging on people. So how was he going to be able to keep his spidey senses in check?

Jesus, Jerry, what have you gotten yourself into? Jerry rolled his neck. *Okay, first things first. I need to know what car the man is driving.* His was the only vehicle under the loading zone. Jerry recalled the suitcase the man had wheeled inside. *He might not be coming back to his car tonight. How am I supposed to know which one's his?*

Jerry closed his eyes, replaying the image. The car was a sedan, dark blue...no, black. Jerry opened his eyes and surveyed the parking lot. *Great, only a half a dozen in the lot that come close to matching.* Jerry moved so he could see the counter. The man was still at the desk chatting up Bev. *Okay, so he's still there. What are you going to do? Excuse me, but I need to know which car is yours so I can make sure you don't get killed.* While some might believe him, most would not.

Jerry moved his Durango to the west side of the parking lot, parking where he could clearly see the front of the building along with Bev's Ford. Lowering the windows, he shut off the engine and brought his palms up, tapping the tips of his fingers together. *Come on, Jerry. Think. How are you going to prevent the man's accident? Easy – fix the situation before it happens. Find out which car the man drives and figure out a way to get the tire fixed before he gets on the interstate. Get that done and you can concentrate on the clerk.* At times like this, Jerry wished he had a tracking device. *Or a dog that was trained to track... Gunter!*

The second he willed the dog to come, Gunter showed up sitting in the seat beside him, wagging his tail. Jerry ruffed the dog's fur and pointed toward the building. "See that man inside?"

Gunter gave an eager whine.

"I need to know which car he's driving." Jerry nearly told the dog the color but stopped – best to be sure.

Gunter disappeared and reappeared just outside the driver's side door.

Jerry got out, and Gunter glued himself to his side as he moved to where he could see inside the building. Once in place, Jerry crouched – whispering so that Gunter could hear. "Don't let them see you!"

Gunter took off toward the building, the doors opened, and he walked inside. As the dog entered, both Bev and the man looked to see who'd triggered the doors. Jerry relaxed when they went back to talking as if nothing was wrong. Gunter circled the man, sniffing. Jerry bit his lip as the man shifted from side to side, readjusting himself as the unseen entity got up close and personal with his crotch.

Gunter moved away, the doors opened, and the ghostly spirit trotted out – his K-9 grin showing him to be vastly enjoying himself. Jerry knew Gunter was triggering the door on purpose, as he'd personally seen the dog walk through walls.

Nose to the ground, Gunter made a beeline across the lot and into the third row sitting next to a late model Buick. Jerry smiled his approval. Not only was the car black, but the hood was also warm to the touch.

"Good job, Trooper." To Jerry's surprise, Gunter jumped up, placing his paws on his chest – further amazed when he ruffled the dog's hair, and Gunter rewarded him with eager whines, sneaking in a lick along his jawline. Jerry wiped his face and looked to see if anyone was watching. *Don't get distracted by all the warm fuzzies, Jer.*

Ordering the dog aside, Jerry took a cursory walk around the car, trying to see if he could locate the faulty tire. Not detecting an issue, Jerry returned to his Durango and drummed his fingers on the steering wheel. "Now what, dog?"

Gunter yawned.

Jerry laughed. "Don't go starting that. We've got work to do."

Gunter tilted his head.

"That's right, work. See that man in there?"

Gunter looked toward the building.

"If we can't figure out a way to stop him, he will get in that car over there tomorrow. Somewhere along his route, he's going to have a flat tire and when he goes to change it, he's going to be killed. And see that woman?"

Once again, Gunter looked to where Jerry pointed.

"She will come outside sometime in the next few hours and be attacked by a man with a knife." Jerry banged the back of his head against the headrest several times. "This is crazy. How am I supposed to help everyone in this city that needs my help and protect Alex?"

Gunter growled a low growl.

"Sorry…we. How are we going to help everyone?"

Gunter yipped a small bark of approval.

"Dog, with that ego, you would've made a great Marine." Jerry leaned his head against the seat. Exhaustion didn't even begin to describe how tired he felt. *Suck it up, McNeal. All you've done is sit on your ass all day. It's not even ten p.m. You had it much worse in the desert.*

Jerry closed his eyes, pulling the images into his mind. The vision showed the man changing a flat tire. *I have to figure out which tire's bad and make it so he needs to get it fixed before getting back on the road.* Jerry opened his eyes, rooted through the glove compartment, and fished out the tire gauge – patting himself on the back for having kept it when cleaning out the old pickup. If he could figure out which tire had the problem, he might be in luck.

"Gunter, I need you to watch my back."

The dog barked and disappeared. Jerry heard a second bark and looked to see Gunter standing outside the Durango. Unlike the moment prior, Gunter was wearing his police collar and the K-9 service vest he wore when he was alive and on patrol with the Pennsylvania State Police. In addition, Gunter was missing the portion of his ear that had been chewed off by a crackhead in the line of duty several years before the dog lost his life jumping in front of a bullet intended for the dog's partner, Trooper Brad Manning.

Jerry blinked his surprise. Gunter normally appeared to him in whole form without a collar or vest. He thought back to when Gunter had materialized to save Savannah during the psychic convention – *Was the dog wearing the vest? Yes, I believe he was. Could it be he knew the difference between working and not working? Would a dog even know the difference? Maybe... if the dog was a ghost.*

Jerry opened the door and got out. "Glad to see you're taking the job seriously."

Gunter growled and wagged his tail.

"Okay, here's the plan. I'm going to check out the tires on that car, and you make sure no one sneaks up on me. There is a guy out here somewhere with a knife. I'd prefer to remain in one piece." Jerry remembered Gunter's missing ear. "No offense."

Gunter wagged his tail, and Jerry took that as a sign the dog didn't harbor any ill feelings.

Jerry made his way across the parking lot, keeping out of sight of the lobby door. He returned to the Durango and pulled on a ballcap, hoping it would help shield his face from any hotel cameras – at least the guy hadn't parked in the front row. With any luck, he would be able to find the faulty tire and help it along, better for the man to delay his trip than to let things play out the way they did in Jerry's vision.

Jerry circled around the back of the car and was about to unscrew the cap on the valve stem when Gunter growled, alerting him to a man and woman exiting the hotel. Jerry scrambled behind the car, waiting as the couple got into an SUV in the front row and left. Jerry approached the car for a second time, stopping once more when a vehicle pulled into the parking lot. Jerry stooped as if to tie his shoe, hoping they didn't look close enough to realize he was wearing boots under his jeans. Suddenly pissed off at the absurdity of the situation, Jerry pulled his knife from his pocket and thrust it into the left rear tire. Pocketing the knife, he returned to the truck, surprised to find Gunter sitting in the passenger seat.

The dog's mangled ear was intact; he no longer wore a collar or vest. Gunter stared at him when he slid behind the wheel, and Jerry had the distinct feeling the dog didn't approve of his actions.

"Don't look at me like that. It was either shank the man's tire or play cat and mouse all night."

Gunter yawned.

"I know we don't know if it was the correct tire. But my spidey senses stopped pinging on the guy, so it worked; just hanging around long enough to get it fixed will give the driver of the other vehicle time to get down the road. He does that, the guy should be safe." *Jesus, Jerry, been off the job for only three days and here you are committing crimes and reasoning with ghosts. Your parents would be so proud.*

Chapter Six

The air lay dormant as a heavy blanket of humidity hugged his skin. Jerry wished for the umpteenth time to be able to turn on the air conditioning, if only for a few moments. Gunter growled. Jerry looked to see Bev step outside. It was the second time she'd ventured outside in the last hour. At first, Jerry thought she was taking a smoke break, but she never lit a cigarette – just stood under the overhang rubbing her hands along the length of her arms.

"It was cool inside the lobby. She's probably coming outside to warm up. Unless she feels something more than humidity in the air."

Gunter gave a slight whine.

Jerry roughed the dog's fur. "Easy, boy, we still have some time yet. Remember, a Marine never gives away his position."

Gunter tilted his head and gave him a look as if asking who Jerry was calling a Marine.

Jerry's cell phone chirped. He looked at the screen, surprised to see a text from Manning asking if he was busy. *10:53 p.m. What the hell, Manning.*

Jerry returned the phone to the console as Bev went back inside. "Any clue why your old partner thinks we're buds?"

Gunter lifted his lip and gave a snarl.

"Fine, I'll be nice. Maybe chatting with the guy will help me stay awake." Jerry picked up the phone and typed his reply. *What's up?* Within seconds, the phone rang. Jerry swiped to receive the call. "What can I do you for, Manning?"

"Hey, McNeal, just wanted to call and check on you. I know we didn't always see eye to eye, but I at least thought you'd make an effort to say goodbye."

Jerry rolled his neck. "I'm not good with goodbyes."

"So I see. Listen, I can't sleep. You want to get a drink?"

Jerry stared into the phone. Six years on the force, and Manning had never asked him to do anything. "Geez, Manning, I'd love to, but I'm in the wind. Matter of fact, I'm in Louisville."

"Louisville, Kentucky? What are you doing there?"

None of your damn business. "Visiting a friend. Came down for the Derby festivities."

Manning laughed. "Never figured you as a horse man."

I'm not. "There's lots to do besides horse racing."

"Cool. Hey, listen, I wanted to tell you this in

person, but thanks for the dog."

Jerry looked over at Gunter. "Dog?"

"Yes, that guy you put Seltzer in contact with came through. I'm getting a replacement for Gunter."

Gunter gave a low growl, and Jerry covered the phone. "Mike's a good guy."

"Good to know. I'll be spending a few weeks in North Carolina working with the dog and learning his routine."

Gunter gave another growl and Jerry pointed a finger to silence him. "You really like having a dog around, don't you, Manning?"

"Yes. But that's not the whole of it. You might not know it, but I'm not the easiest guy to get along with."

Jerry shook his head but refrained from agreeing with the man.

"I guess I tend to rub people the wrong way."

You got that right.

"I wouldn't do good with a human partner, but dogs, they get me."

Jerry lost the smile. Could it be he actually had something in common with Manning? He, too, liked to work on his own but even now found comfort in knowing that even though he was sitting in a dark corner of the parking lot with his windows down, no one was going to sneak up on him. And there was something about walking with a dog at his side that felt…right.

"You still there, McNeal?"

"Yeah, I'm here." *Just having a moment.*

"You got quiet. I thought I'd lost you."

"No, I was just listening to what you had to say."

"Yeah, I tend to ramble on if you let me."

"That's okay, Manning. Shoot me a picture when you get the new dog."

"Sure will. You take it easy, McNeal. Don't lose too much betting on those horses. And McNeal?"

"Yeah?"

"Thanks for taking my call."

"Anytime, Manning." Jerry clicked off the phone and stared at the device. It took a lot for a man to admit his own faults. "Maybe the guy's not so bad after all."

Gunter growled.

"What, I was being nice."

Gunter growled again, and Jerry realized he'd keyed on something. He looked and saw Bev standing near the front of the building, talking on the phone. While he couldn't hear what was said, he could tell by her body language that she was upset. The hand not holding the phone was dancing as if words were not enough to get her point across to the person on the other end of the line. After several moments, she ended the call, slipped the phone into her pocket, and went back inside.

"Yo, dog. You thinking what I'm thinking?"

Gunter tilted his head in response.

"What if this thing that's going to happen isn't random? What if Bev knows her assailant? You saw her on the phone. What if this is a domestic? A husband? Boyfriend? I saw more than one slash mark in my vision. That seems personal. Like the person who did it was angry. That phone call looked angry to me. What do you think? It got legs?"

Gunter yipped.

"Yeah, I think so too. Now what to do with the information?" Jerry tapped his fingers together for several moments before finally getting out and going into the hotel. There was no one at the desk, so Jerry ordered Gunter to guard the desk then went to the bathroom. When he came out, Gunter was standing in front of the counter while Bev worked behind the desk.

She looked up when he neared and he could tell she'd been crying.

Jerry approached the counter. "Everything alright?"

"Excuse me?"

"I couldn't help but overhear your phone conversation." It was a lie, but he couldn't think of any other way to get her talking. He shrugged. "My windows were down."

Tears welled in her eyes. "Oh."

Easy, Jerry, you need her to talk. "I didn't actually hear anything, just saw that you were upset."

"Oh, honey, it's nothing to trouble yourself over. It's been ages since he and I have gotten along."

"He?" This was the guy; he could feel it.

A ripe blush crept up her face. "My son. It's not his fault. It's the drugs."

Shit. Jerry was hoping it was a husband or ex. A son would be a harder sell. No matter how bad things were between her and the boy, she'd likely never believe him capable of hurting her. Not like that anyway. "He live around here?"

"I don't know where he lives. I told him I wasn't going to put up with his shit anymore and he left." Her blush deepened. "Oh, honey. I don't mean to burden you with my troubles."

"It's no burden at all. I understand how boys can be."

She sniffed and wiped at her eyes. "You got a boy?"

Jerry laughed. "Not even a wife. But I used to be one and know what I put my momma through when I was young."

"You look like you've grown up to be a fine young man. I'm sure your momma's proud of you." Tears slid down her face and she batted them away with the back of her hand. "I'm not sure I'll ever be able to say the same about my boy."

Not if he kills you. "Any chance he'll come here tonight?"

Her eyes went wide then she recovered. "No, Ray asked for money for rent, and I told him no. He's sung that song too many times – I give him money and it goes to drugs. I offered to drive him to a shelter but told him he wasn't getting any money. Actually, I think my exact words were 'over my dead body'."

A cold chill washed over Jerry. "Bev, I don't want to alarm you, but sometimes when people are seeking drugs, they do things they might not do if they were clean."

She held up a hand to stop him. "You don't have to tell me that. Why do you think I kicked him out in the first place?"

"He's tried to hurt you before?"

"Hurt me? No, I'm his mother. Ray would never hurt me. Stealing from me is another matter. He'd steal anything that isn't nailed down. He stole my dear mother's wedding rings; God rest her soul. That was the final straw – I'd finally had enough and kicked him out. He begged me to let him stay – swore he'd get his life together and promised to quit doing drugs. I told him to bring the rings back and take weekly drug tests – they have those kits at the drug store, you know – but he'd already sold the rings and couldn't remember who he'd sold them to."

"How long since you kicked him out?"

"Five months and seven days." Bev shrugged.

"What can I say? I'm his mother. I might not like him right now, but I'll always love him."

Jerry felt like banging his head against the wall. Usually, he allowed things to play out. If he interfered, he might not be able to intervene when the time came. *I have to tell her.* Just as he opened his mouth to do so, Gunter clamped his teeth onto his hand, holding on so tight, Jerry felt his eyes water. He tried to pull his hand away and Gunter growled.

Jerry looked at Bev, who remained oblivious to what was going on right in front of her. He forced a smile. "I understand and wish you all the best. I think I'll take that nap now."

"Thanks for listening."

"No worries." The moment they were outside, Gunter released his hold and Jerry studied his hand, looking for puncture wounds. "What the hell, dog?"

Gunter licked his lips and headed for the Durango.

Once inside, Jerry turned to the dog. "Okay, so I take it I wasn't supposed to tell her that her son is coming here to try to kill her. I hope that means you have a plan."

Gunter yipped a playful yip.

"Listen, I'm okay with us working together. As a matter of fact, I kind of like having you around. But in the future, no teeth. That shit hurts!"

***

A cool breeze blew into the cab of the Durango and Jerry welcomed the drop in humidity. He looked at his phone to check the time: two thirty-two a.m. He'd been awake twenty-two hours and had spent most of that time behind the wheel. At least when he was driving, it was easier to stay awake. Gunter sat in the passenger seat, ears alert, his nose twitching with every sound.

A car came into the lot and Jerry pushed back into the seat. The car drove past, and Jerry got a clear look at the female driver within. She drove slowly past the building and then rounded toward the east lot. Gunter remained stoic, watching until the car was out of sight, then turning his attention back to the front of the building. Knowing the dog was on watch gave him comfort. Jerry closed his eyes.

Gunter growled. Jerry opened his eyes to find the dog wearing his police K-9 uniform he'd worn when alive. Instantly awake, Jerry looked toward the building. Seeing nothing amiss, he scanned the parking lot. Jerry touched the dog at the shoulder blades, felt him tense, and removed his hand. "What is it, boy?"

Gunter continued to stare out the front window. Jerry felt the tension as his warning bells told him it was time. He started to get out, then remembered the dome light and thumbed the wheel down to disengage it. He got out, then pushed into the door just enough to hear it click. As he did, Gunter sailed effortlessly out the passenger side window. Jerry hurried to the other side, placing his hand in front of Gunter's nose, telling him to wait.

Bev walked out the front door, heading toward her car. Jerry's heartbeat increased and he scanned the lot once more. This time, he saw a shadow of a man crouched near a car in the center of the parking lot. Jerry started toward Bev. She hesitated then must have recognized him as she began walking once again. As she did, her pursuer moved forward, stalking the woman who'd given him life. Jerry knew better than to call out to the guy, as doing so would alert Bev. He needed her to keep moving forward so he could intercept Ray before he got to his mother.

Jerry increased his pace, feeling as if everything was moving in slow motion. Gunter remained plastered to his side, matching him step for step, while whining his eagerness.

The doors to the hotel opened. The woman he'd seen drive by ran out, waving her hands and pointing toward Ray. "Bev, run, he's here!"

Instead of running, Bev turned, looking behind her. As she did, Ray made his move, running toward his mother, knife raised.

Jerry raced forward. Gunter took off like a shot, whipping around Bev just as Jerry reached her. Gunter jumped in between mother and son. Jerry pulled Bev away, watching helplessly as the blade dipped deep into the dog's side.

Ray pulled back the blade, made another attempt at the dog, and Jerry roundhouse-kicked the knife out of his hand before wrestling him to the ground. He reached for his handcuffs, surprised not to find them at his hip. *You're not a cop anymore, Jerry.* He could hear Bev crying over his left shoulder and the woman who'd alerted her asking if she was okay. He pressed his knee to Ray's back. "Call 911!"

The woman took off running toward the hotel entrance.

Jerry looked for Gunter, but he was nowhere to be found. Jerry swallowed, concentrating on his breathing as his adrenaline slowed. *Gunter's okay, Jerry. You can't kill a dead dog.* He looked over his left shoulder at the clerk. "Are you alright, Bev?"

Bev moved around to where she could see her son. She wrung her hands, her voice trembling as she spoke. "I knew you were angry, but I never dreamed you would try to hurt me."

"I asked you for help!"

"No, you asked me for more money for drugs. You want help? I'll get you help but no more money."

***

It was nearly four in the morning when the police loaded Ray into the waiting police car. Once again,

Seltzer's ruse paved the way for Jerry to sail through on the pretense that he was an out-of-state trooper visiting town. As the patrol car rolled out of the parking lot, the last feeling of unease lifted. Jerry wished the same could be said for Bev, who was racked with motherly guilt. God, he hated to see women cry. "Are you okay, Bev?" He knew she wasn't, but he didn't know what else to say.

"He said he didn't mean to hurt me. He was trying to kill the dog. How could he be so strung out that he thought I was a dog?"

Because he's lying. "Maybe this is enough to get him to take steps to get clean."

"From your lips to God's ears. I'm just glad you were here to stop him. I know my son, and if he had hurt me, he wouldn't ever be able to look me in the eye again. At least now we have a chance of rebuilding our relationship after he gets clean."

All of this and she still can't admit how close she came to dying here tonight. "Happy to have helped, ma'am. If you're good, I think I'll try and get a bit of shut-eye."

Bev pulled out her cell phone. "Listen. It's a long shot but give me your phone number. I'll call you if we get a cancelation."

Jerry rattled off his cell number then walked across the lot to his Durango. As he approached, he had a feeling of being watched. He looked and saw Gunter waiting for him in the passenger side seat.

Jerry's hands came together in prayer form in front of his face, trembling as he gave thanks for the dog's safe return.

Chapter Seven

The phone rang, pulling Jerry from sleep. *Savannah*. He looked at the time: six fifty a.m., less than two hours since he'd put his seat back. He swiped the phone to answer and hit the button to bring the driver's seat up to a sitting position. "Hello?"

"Shoot. Are you still in bed?"

He grabbed the back of his neck and pushed it into his hand. "No, I'm not in bed."

"Good. Are you dressed?"

"Yep."

"Awesome. I'm making breakfast. Are you hungry?"

Jerry glanced at Gunter, sitting in the passenger seat looking bright as the morning sun. "I could eat."

"Great. It will give you a chance to meet Alex."

Jerry sat up straighter. "She's not working today?"

"Not until this afternoon. Today is Thunder."

Jerry looked at the sky. "I didn't know it was supposed to rain."

"Not that kind of thunder, silly. Fireworks. You

70

do like fireworks, don't you?"

"Not really."

"Yeah, right. Everybody likes fireworks."

"Not everyone."

"Well, I'll be there and so will Alex. You said you needed to stay close to her." Savannah's voice became serious. "Have you gotten any more information?"

"To be honest, I've been a little busy."

"Busy? What could be more important than trying to figure out what's going to happen to Alex? You promised, Jerry."

Jerry closed his eyes and placed two fingers at the bridge of his nose. "Listen, I had a rough night and…"

"A rough night? You went out drinking? Jesus, Jerry! I thought I could count on you."

Jerry clicked off the phone and offered it to Gunter. "If she calls back, you answer it."

The phone rang as he clicked his seatbelt into place. Gunter looked at him and yawned. Jerry swiped to decline the call. "And that right there is why I'm not married."

Gunter tilted his head.

"What? You don't approve?" The phone rang once more, and Jerry answered, intending to tell her he was on his way. "This could be construed as harassment, you know."

"It could? I didn't mean to harass you."

Jerry pulled the phone away from his ear and looked at the caller ID. Not Savannah. Maxine, a teenager from Michigan who also had the gift. "Max?"

"Yes, Trooper McNeal?"

He thought about correcting her but decided against it. A few moments on the phone with him and she'd know. "It's early. Are you okay?"

"I wanted to catch you before you went to work." The line went quiet for a moment, and he knew she was reading him. He swiped to turn on the Bluetooth and Max's name showed up on the display. A second later, her voice drifted through the speakers. "You're not going to work anymore, are you?"

"Not with the police force."

"Oh."

"Don't sound so broken-hearted. I didn't get fired. Leaving was my decision."

"How are you supposed to help me if you're not a cop anymore?"

Jerry looked over his shoulder and merged onto the interstate. "Max, is something wrong? Have you gotten any more information on the lady from your dreams?"

"A little. It backed off some, but she still visits my dreams several times a week. I saw her eyes. They're green and I think her name is Virginia. She wants me to help her, Mr. McNeal. How am I supposed to do that if all I know is she has green

72

eyes, and her name is Virginia?"

She was right; it still wasn't enough. "Max, I know it's frustrating, but it's more than you had. Are you still keeping your journal?"

"Yes."

"The key is to jot down your notes the moment you wake up. Make a note of anything you saw, smelled, or heard during the dream."

"I heard a bell."

"Good, make a note of it and anything else you can remember."

"You think the bell might be a clue?"

"It could be. That's why it's important to write everything down."

"I had a dream about you last night. That's why I wanted to call. In my dream, you were looking for a horse with wings. It seemed important."

Jerry swallowed. "Tell me about the horse."

"It was a horse with wings. Does that mean anything?"

He didn't want to scare her, but the kid was good, and he needed all the help he could get. "Yeah, it means something. The horse is a Pegasus and I need to find it."

"I feel like they're all around you."

Damn, she's good. "They are. That's why she's so hard to find."

"The horse in my dream was black."

"That's good to know, Max. Was there anything

else in your dream?"

"Gunter was there. I haven't told anyone about him, Mr. McNeal."

"That's good, Max. Hey, if we're going to be working together, I think you should call me Jerry."

"It's a good thing Gunter's dead."

Jerry looked at Gunter, who was listening to the conversation. "Why is that?"

"On account of the man last night didn't kill him."

Jerry shook his head. "Max, you sure are something."

"That's what I don't understand. I can read you and you're not even here, but this lady keeps coming to me in my dream, and I can't help her."

"I don't begin to know what half of this shit means. Sorry for the language."

Laughter floated through the speakers. "I hear worse than that at school."

"I'm sure you do. Just remember to treat everything like a clue. If you think of something, write it down, no matter how small that something is. Whether it comes to you as a vision or a dream, every detail is a message. Sometimes you won't know the significance of it until the whole puzzle is pieced together."

"Jerry, I just had another vision."

"About the lady with green eyes?"

"No, this one was about you. You're scared. No,

more than scared. Your heart is racing and it's dark. You don't have to be scared, Jerry. Gunter is there and he's big. Towering over you. He's your cloak."

"My cloak?"

"That's the way it feels. Kinda like Superman's cape – when he's wearing it, he can't get hurt. I think when Gunter is with you, it's his job to protect you."

"That's good to know, Max."

"I got to go. Mom's calling me for breakfast."

"Okay, Max, remember the journals."

"I will. Bye."

The call ended and Jerry cast a glance toward Gunter. "First I have spidey senses and now I'm Superman. Don't take this the wrong way, but this superhero status scares the crap out of me."

Gunter growled a deep growl.

Jerry sighed. "You know you're not helping, right?"

Gunter lolled his tongue out the side of his mouth and wagged his tail.

Jerry sighed. "Are you a dog or a comedian?"

***

Jerry got out of the truck, hesitating when Gunter followed. "I think you should find something else to do for a while. They're not going to like it if you upset Cat."

Gunter looked toward the house, back to Jerry, and promptly disappeared. Jerry heard the big white dog barking in the distance and hurried to the door.

When he got there, Savannah was waiting, reminding him of a mother about to scold a child. "I can't believe you hung up on me!"

Jerry rocked back on his heels. "You sounded like my mother."

She raised an eyebrow. "You'd hang up on your mother?"

"Nope. I said you sounded like her, not that you were her."

Alex came up behind her and peeked over her shoulder. Her hair was shorter than what he's seen in the photo. Other than that, she looked the same. She looked him up and down and elbowed Savannah in the ribs. "You going to let him in, or should I arrest him for trespassing?"

Savannah blew out a sigh. "I guess he can come in."

The moment he entered, Alex smiled and extended her hand. "I'm Alex. Savannah has told me a lot about you. I'm in your debt for saving her life."

The moment their hands touched, Jerry felt a jolt. He smiled to cover it but saw Savannah bite at her bottom lip. "Just doing my job."

"Savannah told me you quit and that you might be interested in a job on Louisville PD."

Jerry let go of her hand. "Did she now?"

"I said maybe. I know you're looking at other options. I just thought since you are in town, Alex could get you a ride-along."

That's not a bad idea. It would keep me close to her. Before Jerry could say as much, Alex shook her head.

"My supervisor is not going to go for that this week. Not with everything going on."

"Come on, Alex, it's worth a try and you said it yourself – we owe Jerry for saving my life."

Alex held firm. "They're not going to give permission for a civilian to ride along during Derby Week."

"What if I'm not a civilian?"

Alex looked at Savannah. "I thought you said he quit?"

Jerry answered for her. "Technically, I'm still on the force. My sergeant will vouch for me."

Alex reached in the drawer and handed him the same paper and pen that Savannah had offered him the day prior. "Write down your sergeant's name and number. I'll make a call and see what I can do. Don't get your hopes up; not for this week anyway."

If it's not this week, it won't matter. "Just have your supervisor call that number. My sergeant can be rather persuasive."

Alex walked out of the room to make the call, and Jerry pulled out his cell phone.

"What are you doing?"

"Texting Seltzer."

"Are you sure he'll vouch for you?"

Jerry returned the phone to his pocket. "He

always does."

"You felt something earlier when you shook her hand, didn't you?"

"I did."

"Want to share?"

"There's nothing to share. Same thing as yesterday, a flying horse and a rainbow." He started to add that the feeling had intensified but decided against it. No need to worry her any more than he already had.

Cat came in, sniffed at Jerry's leg, and hissed. Jerry laughed. "Good to see you too, buddy."

Savannah called the feline over and pulled him into her lap, loving on him. "Maybe he smells the dog."

"I don't think Gunter smells. Cat probably thinks I've come to take him back home."

Savannah turned Cat to face her. "Don't you worry, Mr. Snugglesworth. You're staying right here with me and your other mommy."

Jerry arched a brow. "What happened to Gus?"

"It didn't fit him."

"And you think Mr. Snugglesworth does?"

"Just trying it on for size."

Alex returned to the room. "Trying what on for size?"

Savannah held up Cat. "What do you think of Mr. Snugglesworth?"

Alex took the cat from her. "Sounds too much

like syrup. Isn't that right, Mr. Meowgy?"

Jerry groaned. "Shit, I'm sorry, Cat. Maybe I should have kept you."

"Too late," both women said at once.

The timer went off on the stove. Savannah used an oven mitt to remove a casserole dish then hit the button on the coffee maker. "What did you find out, Alex?"

"That your friend here is a hero. He saved a hotel clerk from getting stabbed this morning."

Savannah handed Jerry a cup of coffee, then changed out the pod and hit the button once more. She took out three plates and set them on the table. "I thought you said you went out drinking."

"No, I said I had a rough night. You assumed that meant I was drinking."

Alex laughed. "Savannah assumed something? Never!"

Savannah swatted at Alex, and she ducked.

"My supervisor said you were sleeping in your car."

Savannah whipped her head around. "Why were you sleeping in your car? I told you we had extra rooms."

"What you didn't tell me was there's not a hotel room to be had for a hundred miles."

"Yeesh, I guess I forgot about that. So why didn't you call?"

"Because the second I saw the clerk, I knew there

Sherry A. Burton

was going to be trouble. Then a man came in to get a room, and I knew he was going to die too, if I didn't stay."

Savannah's face paled and she turned away. When she returned with the casserole dish, she'd regained a bit of color. "So, what, you're picking up on everyone in the city?"

Jerry knew why she was upset. He waited for her to scoop some egg casserole onto each plate before answering, then looked at both women in turn. "I'm not a hero. I was just doing my job. I was at the hotel, and it happened that I was faced with two people who I knew were going to die if I didn't help them. What would you have me do, walk away and leave them both to die?"

Alex wrinkled her brow. "My supervisor didn't mention two incidents."

"That's because I convinced them they were connected." He pointed to his plate with his fork. "This egg casserole is good, by the way."

"Thanks, it's a bacon, egg, and cheese frittata. Why did you lie?"

"It was better than telling the police that I slashed the man's tire."

Alex laughed. "And yet you just did. I think I'd like to hear the whole story."

Jerry looked at her. "You asking as a cop or a friend?"

"I'll let you know after I hear the whole story."

Jerry told them everything that happened from the moment Bev handed him the Derby schedule.

Alex tilted her head. "But why tell the police her son slashed the tire?"

"The guy was already in trouble. He had a knife, so his slashing a tire wouldn't be a stretch. If the man had changed the tire, there was a chance he would have driven to his destination on the spare. I couldn't risk it. This way, the car had to be inspected for further damage and photographed for evidence. The guy may have been delayed longer, but according to my radar, he would live to see another day."

Alex nodded her agreement. "If I wasn't married to a psychic, I would think you a nut job."

"And now?"

"I think your reasoning makes sense. But what I don't get is why you stopped the dog from going after the guy. You said it yourself; you knew him to be the right guy. Why not stop it before things got out of hand?"

"Because it would have just delayed what I saw. If Gunter would've taken him down, he would've eventually found Bev and most likely killed her."

"And you don't think that could still happen?"

"Not according to my spidey senses." He winked. "That's what my boss called them. The woman's son told the police he saw the dog. No one else did. I think this incident was enough to get him sent to a rehab center and hopefully get his act together."

Alex looked around the room. "Is the dog here?"

Jerry nodded toward Cat, who was sunning himself near the sliding door. "If he were, that cat would be on top of that curtain rod."

Chapter Eight

Alex came into the kitchen wearing her police uniform. Jerry locked eyes with her, then turned and gave Savannah a subtle headshake. Whatever was going to happen would not be today.

Alex pressed her backside to the sink. "You can't fool me, Jerry. I saw that look."

Jerry swallowed. He hadn't intended to tell Alex she was in danger.

"You miss the uniform."

Jerry relaxed. "You got me there."

"I can't imagine not being a cop. It's all I ever wanted to be growing up."

"Looks like you're living your dream." Jerry felt a twinge of jealousy over the fact that he'd yet to find a clear path to happiness.

"Of course, I don't especially like traffic duty, but I guess someone has to do it."

Savannah grabbed a bottle of water from the fridge and handed it to Alex. "At least you'll get off before the fireworks this year."

"Yep. I'll text you when I'm done, and you can tell me where to meet you guys. And remember to park outside the city and take the bus in – traffic will be crazy downtown. I'll be able to park closer and give you a ride back to your car when the fireworks are over." Alex walked to the other side of the kitchen, removed something from a drawer, and handed it to Savannah before giving her a peck on the lips. "Here are the pins to get into Waterfront Park. Aren't they adorable? I thought they were cute, so I bought an extra one. That, or maybe that psychic shit is rubbing off on me and somehow I knew I'd be needing it."

Savannah opened her palm and closed it again. Though she smiled, Jerry could tell something was wrong. She reached her arms around Alex and gave her a ferocious hug.

"If I would've known I was going to get this kind of response, I would've given them to you last night." Alex looked at Jerry and winked, then turned her attention back to Savannah. "I've got to go. I'll text you when I'm off."

Jerry stayed at the table while Savannah followed Alex to the door. A moment later, Savannah returned and he could see her trembling.

Jerry ran his hand over the top of his head. *Please don't cry.* "Problem?"

Savannah opened her hand for him to see. "You tell me."

Jerry stared at the two rainbow pins showing the head of a horse with wings cradled in the palm of

Savannah's hand. *Pegasus.*

"Don't you have anything to say?"

"They're pretty?"

"Come on, Jerry, I don't need jokes right now. I need answers."

You and me both. "I'd give them to you if I had any."

Savannah grabbed his hand and pressed the pins into his palm. "What do you feel?"

He studied the pins for several moments. "Nothing."

"What do you mean 'nothing'? You're the one who said whatever was going to happen was something to do with a rainbow horse."

"I mean this: these are just a coincidence. I'm getting nothing."

"Then why did she buy rainbow pins when she had so many other options?"

Jerry chuckled. He knew she was on the verge of tears, but he couldn't help himself. "You're kidding, right?"

"This is not funny!"

He reined in his laughter. "Close your eyes."

"Why?"

"Just do it."

She did as he said.

"Okay, picture yourself going to the store to buy the pins. They are hanging on a display on the wall."

"No, they are in a box at the counter."

"Okay, a box on the counter. Inside that box are all colors of pins. Pink, blue, red, green, gold, and rainbow. Out of all those pins, which one are you going to pick?"

She opened her eyes. "I'd pick the rainbow one."

"Why?"

"Because a rainbow symbolizes my and Alex's love?"

"Maybe. But also because it's pretty. You'd pick it out of all of the pins in the box because that is the one that made you smile." He handed her the pins. "Try to relax. Whatever is going to happen isn't going to be today."

"Are you sure?"

"I'd stake my life on it."

She smiled a weak smile. "No offense, but it's not your life I'm worried about."

"I can respect that."

***

In his six years of serving with the Pennsylvania State Police, never had Jerry experienced crowds of this magnitude – even when he'd patrolled Philadelphia, nothing compared to the horde of people currently gathered together in Louisville. While a part of him wished to be in uniform, a bigger part of him was glad he wasn't. If he had been visiting the city looking to further his career in law enforcement, this single event would convince him otherwise.

Not that there was anything wrong with the city. On the contrary, it was rather magnificent. He especially liked the way the interstate cut right through the heart of the town – so close, he could wave to people looking out the windows of some of the most prestigious hospitals around. And how fun is a city where you can get your photo taken with a 120-foot-tall baseball bat that weighs thirty-four tons or encourages you to drink bourbon along the infamous bourbon trail.

What Jerry didn't like were the crowds. One of his shrinks placed the blame on PTSD, but there were no crowds in Iraq. At least not where he patrolled. Another shrink said it was because he grew up in a small town and was never exposed to lofty groups of people. Jerry closed his eyes, picturing the man sitting in the wingback chair, one leg crossed over the other showing his sockless ankles while he meticulously chewed the eraser off the end of his pencil. He should have fired the clown the moment he used the word "lofty" to describe a crowd. It would have saved them both months of useless counseling sessions.

The truth of the matter was he'd never liked being in large groups of people simply because he could not turn off his internal radar. It had been like that since he was born. His mother told him stories of how upset he was every time he was around more than a handful of people. They attributed it to fear of strangers, but as Jerry grew old enough to be mindful of his surroundings, he knew there was more to it.

Bootcamp was particularly troublesome, as he was unable to distance himself from the things that troubled him. But as he got to know his brothers, they became family. He thought about his upcoming family reunion and pushed it aside. He would not be able to decide on that until he solved the problem at hand.

Funny how he preferred his Marine family over some of his blood kin. Most of them anyway. There were a few that got under his skin. Then again, that was true with any family.

"How is it you can look a million miles away when you're standing among so many people?"

Jerry smiled a sly smile. "Just lucky, I guess."

"You're not supposed to disappear, Jerry. You're supposed to focus your radar on Alex."

"I've already told you it won't happen tonight."

"I'm going to get some cheesecake. Want some?"

Not only had they eaten a hearty breakfast, but Savannah had hit seven food trucks since they'd arrived. *She needs an intervention. Maybe, but not by you; women are sensitive about shit like that. Don't do it, Jerry.* "Do you always eat this much?"

Savannah narrowed her eyes. "Now who's

sounding like someone's mother? No, I don't always eat this much. Unless I'm stressed and unless there's cheesecake involved."

"Why don't we take a walk instead? I think Gunter's getting restless with all these people."

"He's a ghost, Jerry. I don't think you're ever going to be able to calm him down. Besides, I'd rather have cheesecake." Savannah pushed her bottom lip out. "I'll get you one too."

"I'll make you a deal. Walk with me to the Lincoln statue and back, and if you still want cheesecake, I'll buy."

"Fine."

Jerry suppressed a laugh. If not for the lack of a foot stomp, she reminded him of a child who hadn't gotten her way. They began walking, Gunter staying close to his side.

Savannah pointed toward the sky. "Look, the air show is starting."

Jerry scanned the sky and saw four biplanes heading their way. "Do you want to stay and watch?"

"No, that's okay. The air show goes on for hours. They will fly right over. The best part is no one can stand in front of you and block your view."

The simple act of walking helped calm his nerves. "This doesn't bother you?"

"What? This?"

"The crowds."

"People? No, I like people. Why, does it bother you?"

Be a man, Jerry. "I've never liked crowds much. It messes with the radar. You're a psychic. I wonder why it doesn't bother you."

"I don't allow it to – at least not when I'm in the moment. Later, I'll be drained, but for now, I'm having fun."

Jerry heard the roar of a larger plane and looked up to see a C5 Galaxy lumbering overhead. He rolled his neck to relieve the tension.

"You good, Jerry?"

"Golden."

"What?"

"Oh, just something me and the guys say. You know, good as gold?"

"Oh."

"Maybe it's before your time."

She laughed an easy laugh. "You're not that much older than me."

They reached the Lincoln statue and Savannah pointed. "Want me to take your picture sitting in his lap?"

Jerry shook his head. "I'm good."

"You sure? It's the thing to do when you're in town."

"I'll pass."

"Okay, then you can take mine." She handed him her cell phone and got in line behind a group of people waiting to have their turn on the statue.

Jerry thought to remind her that she lived here, but a wheezing noise caught his attention. Not a wheeze, but a high-pitched whine of a jet. His mouth went dry as the aircraft neared, the whine turning into a roar. He knew that sound as well as he knew the sound of his own voice.

A-10 warthogs! Take cover, McNeal!

Jerry turned in a circle, staring out at all the people. *Why aren't they running? Can't they hear it?* He opened his mouth to warn them, but nothing came out. Not only couldn't he speak, but he couldn't run. As the jets roared overhead, Jerry closed his eyes. This was it; this was the end.

Something wet touched his hand, and he wondered for a moment if he were bleeding. He felt it again and looked to see Gunter licking his hand. Jerry pulled his hand away. The sky was quiet. *I'm still alive.*

"Jerry!"

Jerry blinked. Focusing on the voice, he saw a woman sitting on the statue looking less than pleased.

"These people are waiting. Are you going to take my picture or what?"

Gunter whined at his side. Jerry heard Doc's voice whispering in his ear. *Get it together, McNeal. Savannah. Not Iraq, the airshow. Shit!*

***

"Are you feeling better?"

Jerry was lying on a blanket they'd stretched over the grass. Gunter lay in a low crouch at his side, keeping a close eye on those around them. Though various military aircraft continued to fly overhead, he had not had any further issues. "I'm fine. I'd be even better if you stop hovering over me."

Savannah sat beside him, wringing her hands. "I can't believe I didn't see what was happening."

"How could you? You said yourself I was just standing there."

"But why didn't I feel it?"

"I'm the last person to ask about that. I'm still trying to figure out my own curse."

"You've saved so many people, myself included. Do you really feel it's a curse?"

Sometimes. "No, I guess not."

"Liar."

Jerry raised an eyebrow. "So now you can read me?"

"We're closer. Maybe that was it. Too many people between us."

"You're probably right. My radar is all over the place, but not connecting with anyone in particular." He regretted the statement the moment he said it. "I told you before, Alex is safe today."

Savannah frowned. "It's been a while since I heard from her."

Jerry closed his eyes. "Two hours is not a long

time. She's working traffic. In case you haven't noticed, there are probably a hundred thousand people in this park alone."

"You owe me cheesecake."

"What?" Jerry realized he'd fallen asleep.

"Cheesecake. You said if I still wanted some when we got back, you'd buy me one."

Jerry pulled his wallet from his pocket and handed her a twenty.

"You want one?"

Jerry returned his wallet to his pants and used his arms for a pillow. "Nope."

"Suit yourself, but don't ask me to share mine."

"I wouldn't dream of it." Jerry closed his eyes once again. He heard voices and opened his eyes, surprised to find it nearly dark.

"Welcome back." Alex sat next to Savannah with a blanket draped around the two of them. She'd changed out of her uniform, opting for jeans and a sweatshirt.

"Alex? When did you get here? How long was I asleep?"

"Hours," Savannah chimed in. "You were asleep when I came back from getting my cheesecake. I was bored, so I used the change to get ice cream. Gunter had his head resting on your chest. He opened his eyes and stared at me as if to say *Wake him and I'll bite you*. I took a picture. Do you want to see?"

Alex's eyes lit up. "I do."

So do I. "Sure."

Savannah thumbed through her phone, turned it for them to see, and sighed. "He's not in the picture."

Alex scrunched her brows together. "I'm beginning to think you two are pulling my leg."

"I wouldn't lie about this and you know it."

"He's real." Jerry looked at Gunter, lying on his side next to him. "Well, as real as a ghost dog can be."

Savanah looked in the same spot where Gunter was lying. "He's a ghost. I guess we shouldn't be surprised he doesn't show up in pictures."

"He showed up in one."

Savannah's eyes went wide. "After he was dead?"

"Yep. The first time Gunter appeared, I was following the feeling, which led me to a snowplow wreck. The whole time I was helping the driver, I knew I was missing something. And the whole time I was at the scene, this dog kept barking and howling his fool head off. It pissed me off because it was in the middle of a blizzard and this dog was obviously in distress. I was agitated that I'd helped the guy and yet the feeling was still so intense. It should have been gone as soon as I saw the man loaded into the ambulance. But it was worse. I yelled at my sergeant – telling him I was going to find that dog and have a talk with its owner. Only I didn't find the dog – I found the car that had careened into the ravine to avoid hitting the snowplow.

"Holly had been down there for hours, and yet when I found her, she was warm. Within seconds of my arrival, she was freezing. When I asked her how she'd managed to stay warm, she told me the dog had climbed in through the windshield and used his body to keep her warm until help arrived. I didn't see any dog and asked her to describe it so I could go looking for it. She got angry and told me I should know what he looks like and kept calling him my dog."

A frown flitted across Alex's face. "Why did she think it was your dog?"

"Because the ID on the dog's tag clearly identified him as a Pennsylvania State Police dog. I saw the photo myself. My boy here is the same K-9 from our station that died a couple of weeks earlier. I still don't know why she was able to capture him on film when no one else has." Gunter lifted his head and wagged his tail.

Savannah beamed. "He's happy to hear you claim him as yours."

"I guess if I have to be honest, I enjoy having him around."

"Wait? So you're saying he's here now?"

"Yes," both Savannah and Jerry answered at the same time.

Alex touched her fingertips to her head then

flicked her fingers outward. "Mind blown. I sure wish I could see him."

Jerry slid a hand down Gunter's back, hoping to allow Alex to imagine Gunter's silhouette. He felt more than knew that Gunter only showed himself to people who either had the gift or had a reason to see him. From the feeling in his gut, he knew Alex would soon get her wish.

Chapter Nine

As the skies darkened, the crowd grew restless. With their heightened energy came an influx of paranormal warning signals that had Jerry on edge. He closed his eyes, remembering a particularly helpful conversation with Doc when he had been on the verge of panic after an intense battle in Iraq. Doc had looked him in the eye and said *Everyone has a built-in coping mechanism. Something they turn to when stressed – biting a lip or chewing the inside of the mouth – or maybe it's biting off fingernails. Drumming the fingers, tapping of the foot; you get the picture. Don't lose it on me now, McNeal. Find that one body movement that will help get you out of your head.* Jerry recalled asking why it had to be a body movement, and Doc said it had to be something that was always there when you needed it. Jerry had jokingly asked what if that body part got blown off. Doc had stared him down and told him: *If that happens, I'll put you back together again.* Jerry's coping mechanism turned out to be a hand placed on the back of his neck or at times ran across the top of his head.

Remembering Doc's words, Jerry placed a hand on the back of his neck to try to calm his nerves. Gunter stayed close, watching his every move. Jerry knew the dog felt his distress. *Easy, Jerry, it's just a few fireworks. You know they're coming. Everything's going to be alright. And what about what happened earlier? You knew there was going to be an airshow? Dammit, this is no time to psychoanalyze yourself. Suck it up, Marine.*

"You're awfully quiet over there, Jerry. Everything okay?"

Just arguing with myself and trying to talk myself down from crazy. Jerry peered at Savannah. "Never better."

"You knew that woman, didn't you?"

"What woman?"

"The one in the wreck. What was her name?"

"Holly. I didn't know her before the accident."

"You sure? I'm getting mixed signals. Like you knew her, yet you didn't."

Alex burst out laughing. "Better watch out, Jerry, my wife is a self-proclaimed matchmaker."

"I'd seen her around town before but hadn't ever talked to her. And I'd appreciate you staying out of my love life." *Because I don't have one.*

"You like her, though. I could tell by the way your face lit up when you said her name. Give me her number and I'll put in a good word for you."

Jerry rubbed the back of his neck. "Remember

this morning when I said you sounded like my mom?"

"Yes."

"Well, you still do." A blast of small fireworks rained into the sky near the far end of the shore, and Jerry turned to the girls. "Okay, the show's over; it's time to go home."

Alex kicked his foot with hers. "If you liked that, get ready. You've never seen a show like this before. Thunder is a bigger draw than the Derby itself."

An *umph* sounded and a single light streaked through the sky as all eyes turned toward the water. A few seconds later, a thunderous boom sounded as the sky filled with a burst of color. *Okay, that wasn't so bad. Remember to breathe, Jerry.* The thought had no sooner come into his head than the entire waterfront sounded as if the city were under attack. Jerry felt his heart rate increase. When Savannah had mentioned fireworks, he thought it would be a normal show. There was nothing ordinary about what was happening here. Explosions came from all directions, near and far, and the crowd responded in turn.

A burst of something shot into the air, reminding him of his time in the desert. Each boom and blast echoed off the bridges and buildings, and he could feel the pressure as the barrage continued without a second's pause.

The city's under attack! Jerry pushed off from

the blanket, running into what was supposed to be the night. Only there was no night. With each bomb, the cityscape lit up, showing the bodies that littered the ground. Jerry picked his way around the bodies. Even in his panic, he knew to be mindful of the dead.

A man in a camo jacket stepped in front of him and yelled something Jerry couldn't hear. It didn't matter. The guy wasn't with his unit or Jerry would have recognized him. Shadows loomed before him – the sky lit up and the shadows became people. So many people. So much noise. Jerry's only thought was to get away.

Enemy fire shot up once more, and he could hear it raining down behind him. Where was his unit? *Not good, Jerry*. Each time the sky lit up, he saw people of all ages, eyes wide as if wondering how to escape. *What are all the civilians doing here? I can't help them all.*

Someone grabbed hold of his arm. He broke free – running away from the people, away from the noise, away from the vise grip that had clamped onto his heart, making it difficult to breathe. *Please let me live to see another day!*

He needed to find cover. The crowd opened up. Suddenly, he was running free on a car-littered street, heading away from the people but not escaping the noise of the bombs so loud they bounced off the buildings and set off car alarms. Something hit his back and he went down, sliding against the pavement. *I've been hit! Please, God, I'm not ready to die.*

Jerry saw an arched entrance to a building. He got up and scrambled into the archway, pressing his back against the wall. *I need to stay alive until Doc finds me.*

Jerry covered his ears with his hands and closed his eyes. Too late, he felt a presence and knew without opening his eyes that his enemy had found him. He stilled and waited for the threat to come closer, then struck out with everything he had, hitting and flailing until his enemy fell on top of him, the weight of the body comforting, as he knew it would help camouflage him from any further attacks.

Sometime later, the bombing stopped, and his panic ebbed. Jerry opened his eyes, surprised to find not the body of his enemy but Gunter lying across him. The dog lifted his head and ran his tongue along Jerry's face. Jerry ran his hands down the shepherd's side and Gunter wagged his tail. Instantly, he recalled Max's prediction and how she'd told him she'd seen Gunter covering him like a cloak. Jerry buried his head in the dog's fur. *Max was wrong – I'm not Superman.*

***

Jerry pulled out his cell phone, intending to call

Savannah, his finger hovering over a different number. He started to call the number, checked the time, and opted to send a message instead, typing two words with hopeful fingers: *You busy?* He stared at the words until they blurred, then hit send, grateful when a moment later, his phone rang.

"You good, McNeal?" Doc asked before Jerry had a chance to utter a greeting.

"Not so much."

"Talk to me."

"This was a bad one, Doc. Maybe the worst one yet."

"Give me the details."

Jerry told him about the incident with the planes, about thinking he was ready for the fireworks and what had ensued.

"What finally pulled you out of it?"

Jerry thought about telling Doc about the dog then hesitated.

"Come on, McNeal, doctor-patient confidentiality, remember."

"Only you're not my real doctor."

"Still counts."

"Doc, what would you say if I told you I'm being haunted?" *There you go, Jerry, no turning back now.*

"Anyone else, I would tell them to call their shrink. You, I'd want to know if it's anyone I know."

Jerry rubbed the back of his neck, debating if he should tell Doc about the guys that had visited him since their demise. He sighed. *One ghost at a time, Jerry.* "No, it's about a ninety-pound police dog who's been hanging around for a while now. When I was running, I felt something hit my back and thought I was done for – I may have even prayed."

"There's a first for everything, McNeal."

"Yeah, well, I've been thinking, and I figure it was the dog who tackled me. I think it was his way of getting me to stop. When I came out of it, the dog had draped itself over my body. Like a – "

"Warming blanket?"

I was going to say "cape." "Yeah. And I think him doing that is what pulled me out."

"This dog, has anyone else seen it?"

Jerry chuckled. "Trying to determine if I'm sane?"

"Let's call it morbid curiosity."

"He's shown himself to a couple of people." Jerry went on to tell Doc about the first time he'd seen the dog and the incidents since. "It was a rough go at first because the dog didn't like me."

"Nonsense: you're the most likable guy I know." Doc's voice was full of sarcasm.

"Yeah, the dog didn't think so." Jerry stopped short of telling Doc what Savannah had told him about the dog being mad at him for trying to send him away. "He growled at me in the beginning, but I think he might like me now."

"I seem to remember you didn't like dogs."

"I don't." Jerry looked at Gunter and sighed. "Or at least I didn't. This one is different. He's a dog but has the attitude of a Marine."

"How so?"

"He doesn't like being told what to do, probably would just as soon fight me as hang out with me, and yet, he's had my back since the moment he appeared."

"Yep, sounds like most of the Marines I've met."

"I've never been able to figure out why he let Holly capture him on film but hasn't shown up on any other cameras or videos. She showed me the film, so I know it to be true."

"Maybe that's why."

The street was filling as people began to make their way out of the city. "I'm not following you, Doc."

"Maybe it wasn't to convince the girl. Maybe he knew getting her to see him was the only way to convince you. Let's face it, if the dog were showing himself only to you, you'd be questioning your own sanity about now."

"Doc, that train left the station a long time ago."

Doc's laughter floated through the phone. "McNeal, you may be a lot of things, but crazy isn't one of them."

"Thanks for calling me back, Doc."

"Anytime, my brother. You good, McNeal?"

"Golden, Doc."

Jerry had no sooner returned his phone to his pocket than it rang. He pulled it out and saw Savannah's name light up the screen. "Hello?"

"Jerry, where the heck are you?"

Jerry looked around for a street sign and didn't see one. "The hell if I know."

"Where'd you go? One minute we were watching fireworks, and the next, you were running off into the crowd."

"Coffee."

"You went for coffee?"

"Nope, I went in search of a bathroom because I drank too much coffee earlier. I was going to use a tree but didn't want your wife to arrest me for indecent exposure."

"Why didn't you come back?"

"I got turned around and couldn't find you." Jerry was glad he wasn't talking to Max, who would have known he was lying as the words left his mouth. "From the looks of the traffic in the streets, we're not going anywhere for a while. I'll try looking for you again."

"Wait, I have a better idea. Meet us at the Lincoln statue."

"Works for me." Jerry slid his phone into his pocket, waited for an opening in the steady stream of people, and began making his way back to the park. As he walked toward the river, he thought about a video he'd seen on the National Geographic

Sherry A. Burton

channel about salmon spawning and swimming upstream. Suddenly, the stream of people parted, giving Jerry a clear path – it was then he realized Gunter had moved in front of him, clearing the way.

Chapter Ten

A few short weeks ago, Jerry had never even watched a TikTok video, yet here he was sitting alone in the dark living room watching video after video. Not any video, mind you – Jerry was watching dog videos, preferring those that focused on training. He'd already saved countless videos and now found himself comparing the dogs in the videos to Gunter. A video came on that showed a German shepherd opening the front door with his paw. "Oh yeah, well, I'd like to see your dog walk through walls."

"You okay there, McNeal?" Alex didn't wait for a reply as she continued on to the kitchen.

Jerry fumbled to swipe the app closed, then shoved the phone between his legs much like a school kid caught playing with his cellphone well past his bedtime.

When Alex returned to the room, she carried two single-serving tubs of ice cream. She handed him one along with a spoon, then switched on the lamp and climbed into an oversized chair on the opposite side of the room. Wearing pajama shorts and an oversized top, she tucked her bare feet under her bottom as she pulled the lid from her container.

He lifted the lid and spooned out a bite, enjoying the rich taste of chocolate. *Be careful, Jerry. Something tells me you're about to get interrogated.*

She took a bite and pointed the spoon at him. "What's your deal, McNeal?"

Yep, she's in cop mode – handing out a treat to appear non-threatening while asking questions. He took another bite. "I'm not sure I get your drift."

"You show up at our door under the guise of dropping off a cat. And now here you're sitting alone on my couch sounding like a basketball parent who's mad their child didn't get to play in the game."

Jerry pushed the spoon into the frozen dessert. "Does my being here bother you?"

"I just want to know why you're here, and don't give me that BS about looking for work."

She was a good cop – she'd seen right past the ruse. "Why do you think I'm here?"

"We're not doing that." Cat climbed into the chair with Alex and attempted to sniff the container. Alex placed a drop of what looked to be strawberry onto the lid and set it on the table next to her. Cat sniffed it briefly before deciding to indulge in the creamy sweetness.

"Doing what?"

"This cop shit – answering a question with a

question."

Jerry lifted his spoon and took a bite while contemplating his answer.

Alex surprised him by continuing. "My wife may have bought your story about going to the can, but I saw your face and watched you bolt like a scared rabbit. Savannah said you were in the Marines. I'm assuming that was a PTSD episode."

Jerry stiffened in his seat. *Don't lie, Jerry – she'll see right through it.* "It was."

Alex placed her container on the table beside her chair. "I'm assuming you knew the risk when you went."

"I prepared myself beforehand and thought I had it under control."

"Savannah told me you had an episode when the planes flew over. Why didn't you leave then?"

Jesus, now she's trying to play therapist. "As I said, I thought I was prepared."

Alex laughed. Aside from giving him the ice cream, it was the first hint of a friendly conversation since she'd entered the room. "Nothing prepares you for Thunder over Louisville."

"That is no shit. Listen, I've been to fireworks shows since getting out of the Marines. I even worked a few events when I was with the state police. What you guys put on here is more in line with Armageddon."

"I'll take that as a compliment to our city. Now

back to the original question as to why you're here. What's your angle, Mr. McNeal?"

Good work, Alex. I see detective in your future. Jerry sat back in his chair, debating his answer. He worried over telling her about the danger he saw her in, but the option was to lie and tell her he had a thing for her wife, which wouldn't help his case. Better tell her the truth and deal with the consequences. "I'm here to help you."

He expected her to laugh. She did not. "What kind of danger am I in?"

"Does that mean you believe me?"

This time, Alex laughed a hardy laugh. "I figured it was either that or my wife is pregnant, which we both know not to be the case. I hope this is over soon for Savannah's sake."

Jerry was impressed with Alex's calm exterior. "You're not worried?"

"I put my life in danger every time I put on that uniform. Besides, you did okay by my wife, so I figure I could be in worse hands. I will be in uniform when it goes down, right?"

"Good guess."

"Not really. I knew something was up when Savannah asked for me to set up the ride-along."

"And yet you said nothing."

"I wanted to be sure. So where do we go from here?"

"Normally, I would say we continue doing what

we were doing but now that you know, I would like to stay on your six."

"Meaning?"

"Until whatever is going to happen takes place, we stay together. You leave the house – I go with you."

"I thought you said I would be in police uniform."

Jerry brought his fingertips together and flexed his palms in and out several times. "I don't usually broadcast my feelings to the intended target. Now that you know it might change things and I don't want to leave anything to chance."

"Target? Are you saying I might get shot?"

Maybe. "I don't know. Everything is still fuzzy."

"Is that normal?"

"It's part of the process."

"Do you always win?"

No. Don't tell her that. "I'm pretty good at my job."

"Are you still working for the Pennsylvania State Police?"

"Technically, no."

"And yet the database says you are."

Jerry sighed. "It's complicated."

"Uncomplicate it."

"Have you ever thought about becoming a detective?"

"Does it show?"

"A little." Jerry rubbed the back of his neck, trying to decide how much to tell. He wasn't worried about his own ass, but Seltzer would get in a lot of trouble if anyone learned of his part in Jerry's get-out-of-jail-free card. "Listen, I appreciate your tenacity, but I'd like to request an attorney."

"You're not under arrest."

"No, and I'd like to keep it that way."

"Will your secret help you save me?"

"It got your supervisor to agree to a police ride-along, didn't it?"

Alex yawned. "Okay, I'm heading back to bed. You should try to get some sleep. If you're planning on being my shadow, you're going to need it."

"I've done my share of traffic."

Alex pushed off the couch. She shooed Cat away and retrieved the empty ice cream cartons. "Who said anything about traffic?"

***

The second Jerry woke, he knew someone was in bed next to him. Afraid to move, he searched his mind for answers. He hadn't seen Savannah since she'd gone up to bed. Alex? Not likely, as she had gone upstairs before him. He swallowed. *Unless I climbed into the wrong bed.* He eased toward the edge of the bed, intending to sneak out of the room. The person lying next to him let out a soft moan. *Shit.*

He turned, expecting a confrontation, and Gunter

rolled over onto his back, extending his feet into the air. The dog opened his eyes and wagged his tail.

Jerry pulled on his jeans, thankful he wasn't about to get shot. "I thought we agreed you were not supposed to come inside."

Gunter yawned.

"You can't be tired. You're a ghost. Ghosts don't get tired – do they?"

Another yawn.

"Fine, you can stay but only in here. You're not to scare Cat. He seems to like it here." Jerry pulled on his shirt and left the room, shutting the door behind him. He stood there for a moment staring at the door, half expecting Gunter to follow.

Jerry turned, surprised to see Alex dressed in mesh shorts and a tank top. She lifted a pair of running shoes for him to see. "Problem?"

Jerry jabbed a thumb toward his bedroom door. "I have company."

Alex's brows lifted.

Jerry shook his head. "Not that kind of company. Gunter's in the room."

Alex stepped in front of him, opened the door, and heaved a sigh. She shut the door and looked at Jerry. "A girl can hope, can't she?"

Jerry gave a nod to the shoes. "You're not going to work today."

"We," she gave a wink, "are undercover today."

"Undercover?"

"Yes, I signed up to represent the police force in today's race."

"I'm afraid I'm not following you."

"Oh, you'll be following alright. Especially if you plan on wearing jeans."

They were going to be running in a foot race. He hadn't so much as jogged since leaving Chambersburg. Jerry ran a hand over his head as the implications set in.

Alex looked him up and down. "You do run, don't you?"

"I do. Just give me a moment to change."

"Wear something you don't mind getting ruined."

Jerry arched a brow. "Just what kind of race is this?"

Alex winked. "The kind where people don't mind getting dirty."

"Sounds more like a hockey game than a race."

"Just put on something old and meet me downstairs and tell the dog he'd better not scare Mr. Meowgy."

"I told him, but I can't make him listen." Gunter lifted his head when Jerry came into the room but didn't show any signs of getting out of bed. Jerry rooted through his duffle bag and pulled out a shirt. It wasn't exactly old, nor was it one he'd miss if it met an early demise. He changed into the shirt and running shorts and traded his boots for sneakers.

Gunter lifted his head, cocking it to the side.

"Seems we'll be running in a race today. Alex said people are likely to play dirty. Maybe you should wait this one out."

Gunter lifted his lip and gave a slight growl.

Jerry held up both hands. "Okay, have it your way, but you can't say I didn't warn you."

***

Jerry walked into the kitchen, saw Alex bleeding from what looked to be several stab wounds, and immediately sprang into action – pushing Savannah out of the way and barking orders. "Call 9-11 and grab me some bandages. Towels, blankets, anything that will stop the bleeding."

Savannah laughed. "If you do anything to mess up my handiwork, I'll brain you."

Jerry was appalled. All this time, he'd been worrying about protecting Alex and the threat was right under his nose. Then why wasn't his radar triggered? Even now, his spidey senses idled at a dull roar. He looked at Savannah, who was standing there holding a pair of scissors. "Why?"

"For the zombie run, I thought Alex told you."

Zombie run? He glanced at Alex. "This is all a joke?"

Alex gave Savannah a high five. "Not an intentional one, but it played out rather well."

115

Jerry was incensed. "Played out. You're both lucky I didn't see Savannah with the scissors when I saw you bleeding. This could have gone bad in so many ways."

"Geez, Jerry, lighten up. We weren't intentionally trying to get a rise out of you. We thought you'd laugh, not go berserk."

"Yeah, well, you try having the guys you serve with blown to pieces in front of your eyes. Maybe there's a limb missing, and there's nothing you can do but try to stop the bleeding until help arrives." *Easy, Jerry, they didn't know it would set you off.*

Savannah lowered the scissors. "I'm sorry."

Alex nodded her agreement. "Me too. We didn't mean any harm."

"On the bright side, your wounds look real." Savannah held up the scissors. "Your turn, Jerry."

Jerry shook his head. "I'll pass."

Alex took the scissors from Savannah and faced Jerry. "Sorry, but no deal. The plan is to blend in."

"I'm wearing running gear."

"Yes, which makes you look like a runner, not a zombie."

Jerry smiled. "That's because I'm the real guy, and I'll be in the front of the pack. You know, the guy the zombies are chasing."

"Nice try. Since you haven't been training for a five-mile run, we will have to make you look the part." Alex took hold of Jerry's shirt and began cutting. After several slices, she motioned for Savannah, who added a few strategic wounds to Jerry's skin.

Jerry let out a sigh. All this because he didn't have the heart to abandon an abandoned cat.

Chapter Eleven

Jerry found it weird being chauffeured around, especially when the one doing the driving was a female. He had offered to drive, but Alex insisted on taking the lead, claiming she didn't want to chance changing anything. While this was sound reasoning, Jerry also figured Alex to be just as uncomfortable sitting in the passenger seat as he. She was a cop. Cops liked to be in control. He smiled inwardly, wondering how calm she'd be if she knew Gunter was in the back seat, peering over her shoulder.

They came to a red light and Alex looked at him. "You're quiet, McNeal."

She was back in cop mode, using his last name. "Just trying to figure you out."

"Ah, the tables are turned. What do you want to know?"

"You didn't tell Savannah that you know."

"Nope."

"Why not?"

"Her knowing is bad. Her knowing that I know would be even worse."

"How so?"

The light changed, and several people continued through the redlight. Alex pounded the steering wheel with her fist. "Hello? Cop sitting right here!"

Jerry cleared his throat. "You might have more credence if you were actually driving a police car."

She ignored his quip. "Because if she knew that I know, she'd want to talk about it."

"And that would be bad?"

Alex glanced in his direction. "You've met my wife, right?"

Alex was right. Savannah was worried enough for the three of them. A car stopped in front of them, and Jerry pushed on the brake he didn't have.

"Don't worry, McNeal; I'm not going to let you get hurt." She looked at him and grinned. "I need you in one piece so you can save my ass."

"Why a cop?"

"Why a cop what?"

"You said you'd always wanted to be one. Why a cop?"

She answered so quickly, it was obvious she'd given the question a lot of thought. "I've always been the square peg. When other girls were wearing dresses, I had my ball cap on backwards. My friends wanted to be cheerleaders. I wanted to take things apart to see how they work. One day, a cop came to our school. Nothing bad – just one of those career day things. He was showing pictures on a PowerPoint, and he paused the frame and said, 'This could be you someday.' I swear, McNeal, it looked like the man was staring into my soul. I took the bait. From that day forward, it was all I ever wanted to do. I guess I figured if I were a cop, I'd have some control over my life."

"How's that working out for you?"

Alex blew out a sigh. "Pretty damn good until you came into the picture."

"I could leave."

"Nah, I think it's best you hang around. I wouldn't want to be responsible for your death."

Jerry eyed Alex. "My death?"

"Sure thing. If I send you away, I get killed. If that happens, Savannah would hunt you down like a dog."

"I guess I'd better hang around for a bit and see that you stay alive."

"Reckon that'd be the best plan." Alex pulled up to a parking lot marked "reserved," flashed her badge, and waited for the attendant to pull back the barrier to allow them entrance. They'd no sooner parked when Alex pointed to the street. "Check it out. Here come some of the runners."

Jerry looked to see a group of zombies walking across the street. Arms stretched in front, they dragged mangled legs and looked much like the cast of *The Walking Dead*. "If they all move like that, the race is in the bag."

"Don't let their theatrics fool you. This is just the

pre-race show of those hoping to get their pictures in the newspapers. There's a lot of bragging rights to be had – especially if the winner gets his picture on both the website and front page of the *Courier-Journal*."

Jerry glanced down at his ripped shirt and fake wounds.

"Chin up, McNeal. We're not here to win. We're here to blend in and take action if need be."

Jerry followed Alex to the back of the car, where she pulled a fanny pack out of the trunk and buckled it around her waist. "And if we need backup."

She unzipped her fanny pack to let him peek inside – ID, badge, a small service revolver, and a whistle.

"Where's my fanny pack?"

"You're not a fanny pack kind of guy." She tried to fit her cell phone in the pack, but it wouldn't work, so she powered it off and left it in the trunk.

Deciding he could do without his for a couple of hours, Jerry did the same then rolled his neck.

"Problem, McNeal?"

"No gun, no cell phone. I'm beginning to feel a bit emasculated."

Alex beamed. "I've got your back."

"I'm not used to being a kept man."

"Relax, it's just for a few hours. Besides, you said it's not happening today."

"It's not."

"Then relax and try to have a little fun."

As they began walking, Jerry felt Gunter's presence. He started to acknowledge the dog and nearly tripped over his own two feet. Gunter looked very much the part of a zombie dog. The ear that had been bitten off years earlier by a crackhead was ripped and hanging by a flap of skin. The area where he'd been shot looked fresh and exceptionally gory. There was a second bullet hole along with a knife wound. *Those happened since his return from the dead.*

Alex stopped to see what had detained him. "Are you – Jerry, it's the dog! He's real!"

What!? "You can see him?"

Alex nodded, her face ghostly white. "He looks – God, is he alright?"

Gunter lifted his lips and wagged his tail.

"He's fine."

"Wait, did he just smile?"

"Did I forget to mention he's a comedian?"

"Why is he allowing me to see him? You said he only lets people see him when they're in danger."

Or when he wants to be the star of the show. Jerry gave a chin jut, telling Alex to turn around. A man with a press badge hurried toward them, holding a camera with a high-powered lens.

"Cool makeup!" the reporter called. "Hold up. I want to get a picture of the three of you."

"I guess I'm not the only one who can see him,"

Alex remarked.

"Apparently not. Don't let him get too close. I don't know how Gunter will respond."

Alex dug into her fanny pack and pulled out her badge. "This is a working dog. That's close enough."

The reporter scratched his head. "That's awesome. I didn't know Louisville PD had such a great sense of humor. Can I take a photo?"

Jerry rubbed his hand over his head. "You can take one, but don't be surprised if it doesn't turn out."

The reporter looked through the camera and adjusted the lens. "Oh yeah, why's that?"

"Camera shy. Many have tried, most have failed." Alex turned away and he knew she was trying to keep from laughing.

"Challenge accepted." He held the camera to his eye once more and snapped several photos. "Man, that is some wicked good makeup. It looks so real. I need to get a close-up."

Gunter growled a warning when the man took a step closer.

The reporter halted his advance. "Okay, no close-ups, but you have to at least tell me how you got him to hold still long enough to apply the makeup."

"It's a new process." Jerry shrugged. "I'm afraid I can't give away our secret until the patent comes back."

"That's too bad. People would kill to have their dog looking like this."

"That's what I'm afraid of."

"What?"

Alex grabbed Jerry by the arm. "He said we're going to miss the race if we don't get a move on."

"Okay, one more before you go. Just the dog this time." The reporter pulled an older camera from his bag. Jerry recognized the camera, as it looked just like the one Holly used. The reporter aimed the camera at Gunter. "Fantastic. Oh, just one more question. I know you can't tell me what makeup you used, but how easy is it to apply?"

Jerry touched the top of Gunter's head. "That's the thing with this stuff – it disappears in a flash."

"So it dissolves?"

"Into thin air."

Alex elbowed him the moment the guy turned away. "You enjoyed that as much as the dog did."

"I'd enjoy it more if I could be there when he discovers the dog isn't in any of the pictures."

"Are you sure he won't be?"

Jerry ran both hands over his head and continued along the back of his neck. "When it comes to this dog, I'm not sure of anything."

***

The race began promptly at nine a.m., all zombie limping and limb-dragging forgotten as the runners tore off like someone had lit a match under them. When the crowd in front of them cleared, Alex started a steady jog. Jerry found himself both pleased and disappointed. While he didn't have any aspirations of winning, he at least thought he'd finish in a respectable place.

"You look disappointed, McNeal."

"Not at all. I love finishing last."

"Remember, we're on the job. The goal is to hang back and blend in with the crowd."

"What about the crowd ahead of us?"

"There are people in place for that."

Why couldn't I be partnered with them?

"I heard that."

No way. "You did?"

"No, but I had you for a moment."

Since he was running slow enough to talk without gulping for air, he decided to take advantage of it. "How did you and Savannah meet?"

Alex's lips curved upward. "I went to a psychic show. Saw her across the room and waited my turn to sit at her table."

Sounds familiar. "Let me guess, love at first sight."

"On my part."

"But not on hers?"

"She was in denial."

A runner with his clothes torn to shreds pushed between them, sending Alex stumbling to keep her balance.

Jerry shaped his hand into a gun, pretended to shoot the man, and blew on the end of his finger.

Alex moved beside him again. "Feel better?"

"A little." Jerry frowned at Gunter. "Don't let that happen again."

"She seems happy, so you must have changed her mind."

"Are you digging for details?"

"Nope."

"Good, because you're not getting them." She grinned.

"What's so funny?"

"I was remembering one of our early dates. I was running in a 10K, and Savannah decided to join me."

"Don't take this the wrong way, but I can't see Savannah running in a race."

"She didn't run. She decided to find a place along the route and give me water."

"That works."

"In theory. You see, she's not a runner, so she didn't know how things work. I'm running – really running – and I wanted to impress her, so I was actually trying to set a decent pace. And I see her in the distance sitting at a table at an outdoor café off to my right. She has the water in front of her and I was like, cool, I'm parched. I thought she'd come to the sidelines so I could get a drink. Only she just sat at the table in the courtyard and watched opened-mouthed as I kept going."

"She expected you to stop and get it?"

"She did. Was a bit pissy about it, in fact, asking why I didn't stop to get a drink when she'd made it a point to be there waiting for me."

"What did you tell her?"

"That I was running a race."

"Did she get over it?"

"She said she did, but she never watched me race again."

Another runner pushed between them, elbowing Jerry as he passed. Jerry looked to see Gunter, who was nowhere in sight. An instant later, the dog ran in front of the same runner who tried to stop but ended up toppling over the dog.

Alex started to stop. Jerry grabbed her arm, pulling her forward. "Leave him. He finds out the dog's with us and he'll threaten to sue the city."

"You good, McNeal?"

"Aside from the fact I just got passed by a zombie?"

"You didn't expect to win the race, did you?"

Jerry wiped the sweat from his face. "I'd settle for not coming in dead last."

"I think I can agree with that. What say we pick up the pace a bit?"

"You lead and I'll follow."

Chapter Twelve

Savannah was waiting by the door when they returned. It was clear from the crease between her eyebrows she was upset. Jerry followed Alex inside and kicked off his shoes without untying them. *Don't make eye contact, Jerry. Whatever is going on is none of your business. Just go upstairs and leave them to hash things out in private.*

Savannah stepped in front of him, blocking his way. "Not so fast, Jerry."

Shit! What did I do? Jerry searched his mind but couldn't think of anything.

Alex stooped to untie her sneakers, and Jerry guessed she was having the same internal conversation. She removed her shoes and placed them in the tray by the door before turning her attention to Savannah. "Babe, you seem upset. What's the problem?"

"What's the problem? The problem is I tried to call you a hundred times. Why didn't you answer your cell?"

"Because it's in the trunk of the car."

Savannah narrowed her eyes. "What the hell is it

doing in there?"

Alex chuckled. "It wouldn't fit in my fanny pack."

"This is not a laughing matter!" Savannah turned and pointed her index finger at Jerry. "What's your excuse?"

Savannah crossed her arms, and Jerry resisted the urge to tell her she was giving off the mom vibe again. He didn't know why she was so mad – nor was he picking up on any clues on his internal radar – but it was obvious something had lit a fire under the girl. "My excuse for what?"

"For not answering my calls."

Alex answered before he had a chance – staying calm and choosing her words so as not to exacerbate the situation. "Listen, babe. I know you've been under a lot of stress lately. I'm sorry I missed your calls, but you need to chill. I don't know what you think is going on between me and Jerry, but the answer is nothing. We were at the race. I had to decide what was more important: my cell phone or my gun. I chose my gun. As for Jerry, he didn't have any pockets, and it was easier to leave the phone in the trunk than to carry it in his hand while running five miles. Could we have checked them when we were done? Yes. That's on us. To be honest, when the race was over, our only thoughts were to get out of there before traffic got any worse. That's the whole of it. If you don't believe me, go check the trunk and see for yourself."

Savannah stood with her mouth agape.

Jerry was at a loss for words. *Could that really be the root of Savannah's anger, that she thought they'd spent the day fooling around?* Savannah took in several deep breaths, and for a moment, he thought she was going to cry.

Instead, she surprised him by squaring her shoulders. "First, I'm insulted that you think I don't trust you. Second, I was not trying to check up on you. I was worried about you."

The lines in Alex's face softened. "You knew I was with Jerry. If anything was going to happen, he would be the first to know, right?"

Savannah slid a quick glance to Jerry then returned her attention to Alex. "That is exactly why I was upset."

Alex closed her eyes, then opened them once again. "It's been a long day. We both ran five miles, need to take a shower, and I don't know about Jerry, but I'm hungry. You're going to have to be clearer than that."

Savannah pulled her cell phone from her pocket and swiped the front of it several times before turning it around. "Is this clear enough for you?"

Jerry looked at the phone, then snatched it from Savannah's hand, zooming in on the photo that showed Gunter in all his mangled glory along with the bold headline, **Zombie Dog Wins Big at Derby**

City Zombie Race!

"I saw this and knew it was Gunter. My first reaction was being pissed off that he allowed someone else take a photo, and yet the one I took showed nothing. Then I remembered what you'd said about him only showing himself when there was trouble – I tried calling Alex, and when she didn't answer, tried to call you. When you didn't answer, my mind thought of all the reasons neither of you answered. The more I tried to calm myself, the more I thought of different reasons. I'm not a psycho. I have good reason to worry." The tears had begun. Savannah looked at each of them before finally settling on Jerry. "I can't keep this in anymore. We have to tell her."

Alex stepped forward and wrapped her arms around Savannah. "I already know. Jerry told me. Don't blame him. I knew something was up by the way you were acting. Nothing happened today. I should have texted you before I turned off my phone. I'm so sorry to have worried you."

They stayed embraced for a moment before Savannah pulled away. She sniffed, wiped the tears from her eyes, then looked at Jerry. "You said it could change things if you told her."

Jerry nodded. "That's why I insisted on going with Alex today. My radar told me she would be fine, but I wanted to make sure."

"What about the photo. You said Gunter only

shows himself to people who need to see him." Savannah whipped her head around, looking at Alex. "Wait, does this mean you got to see him?"

Alex nodded. "I did, although I must admit I didn't expect him to look like that."

Savannah shook her head. "He doesn't. Not when I've seen him anyway. Was it makeup or real blood?" Savannah tilted her head as if considering. "It would have to be real blood unless there are makeup artists in the other realm. But why would he appear like that? Was he in pain? I mean, he's dead, so it probably didn't hurt. Tell me he wasn't in pain."

Jesus, he almost preferred Alex's interrogation. Jerry ran a hand over his head. "It was real alright. Near as I can tell, he appeared showing every wound he's received both while living and dead. The ear that had been chewed off by the crackhead, the bullet that killed him. Even the bullet he took when protecting you and the knife wound he got from Bev's son. He was dead when he got the last two and yet somehow was able to manifest those wounds on his body today."

"But why?"

Jerry hesitated. The only answer he had sounded crazy even to him. "I think he did it as a joke. He saw everyone walking around looking like zombies and wanted to fit in. I swear, at one point, he even smiled."

Alex bobbed her head in agreement. "It's true. I

saw it."

"But why even show himself in the first place? You said he only shows himself when the person is in danger."

"That's been the case, until now."

Alex spoke up. "Maybe he likes the attention."

Savannah laughed. "You know this all sounds absurd, right?"

Jerry forwarded himself the photo and handed Savannah her phone. "Not any more absurd than him coming back from the dead in the first place."

"Where is he now? Is he okay?" Savannah realized what she'd said and laughed for the first time since they'd entered. "I mean, as okay as a dead dog can be."

Jerry motioned toward Alex. "Your wife hurt his feelings."

Alex puffed her chest. "I didn't mean to."

"The moment she used her cop voice, he tucked his tail and disappeared."

Alex looked at Savannah as if begging her to take her side. "The dog was a mangled mess, but it wasn't like he was in danger of dying, so I told him he was not getting in my car covered in blood."

"Poor, poor doggy." Jerry looked at Alex and winked.

Savannah wrinkled her nose. "You stink."

Alex jutted her chin. "Okay, I suck. But I wasn't going to let that dog in my car with all that blood over him."

Savannah waved her hand in front of her face. "I didn't say you suck. I said you stink –you both do."

"Far be it for me to offend." Jerry headed toward the stairs. As his foot touched the bottom step, he pondered the photo once more. "The photographer used an older camera."

Both Savannah and Alex answered him at once. "What?"

Jerry walked back to where they stood. "You said you were angry that Gunter didn't show up in the picture you took with your phone. That's the reason. The reporter took multiple photos of the two of us with Gunter. But he only took two of him by himself, and both were taken with an older camera. When he pulled it out, I remember thinking the camera looked like the one Holly used. Maybe it has to be a special kind of camera."

Savannah nodded her head. "I guess that could be the case. It still sucks, as my cell phone is supposed to take the best pictures."

Alex grinned. "I guess they didn't think to test it on ghosts before they made that claim."

"I don't know if I'm right. It could just be a fluke." Jerry caught a whiff of himself and headed up to his room without another word. The moment he entered the bedroom, he felt Gunter's presence. "I know you're here – I can feel you."

Gunter appeared in front of him in full form.

"I'm glad to see you. However, I don't know how I feel about your showing everyone your battle wounds. I sure hope that doesn't come back to haunt me."

Gunter moved to a lounging position, cocked his hip to the side, and placed his head between his front paws, staring up at Jerry with disapproving eyes.

"You're right. That was in poor taste. I have to admit – you make a damn good zombie. And cutting in front of the jerk like you did was pretty cool too. I guess what I'm trying to say is, for a dog, you're pretty alright."

Gunter lifted his head and wagged his tail.

***

Jerry was just about to head downstairs when he received a text from Max.

I drew this for you. Jerry clicked on the attachment, surprised to find an impressive illustration of a German shepherd materializing from within the clouds and running toward a man. Jerry sat on the bed, staring at the photo. Max had not only visualized his panic attack before it happened, but she'd also seen Gunter protecting him when he was too weak-minded to protect himself. Jerry looked at the picture once more. The dog was a giant compared to the man, who stood watching as the dog ran toward him. Though Jerry could only see the man's back, his body language showed him to be unafraid. *What are you trying to tell me, Max? That*

I shouldn't be afraid of the dog or that there's no need to be frightened when the dog is near?

Jerry canceled out of the photo and thumbed a message to Max. *Thanks for the amazing picture. You are very talented.*

<Max> *Glad you like it. It came to me in a dream. I think it is the dog's way of telling you that you don't have to be afraid when he's with you.*

<Jerry> *I think you're right.*

<Max> *Tell Gunter I said hi.*

Jerry looked at the dog. "Max said to say hello."

Gunter wagged his tail.

<Jerry> *I just did. He said to tell you hello too.*

<Max> *Did he really talk?*

Jerry read her text and smiled. > *No, but he did wag his tail.*

<Max> Cool. But it would've been even cooler if he actually talked.

<Jerry> *I agree. I've got to go for now.*

<Max> *Okay. Glad you liked my picture. See ya.*

Gunter jumped onto the bed beside him. Jerry pulled out his phone, attempting a selfie with Gunter. When he looked at the phone, he was the only one in the frame.

Jerry bumped against the dog, who felt as real as any other dog would. "Just checking."

Gunter gave Jerry a quick lick along his jawline as if to say *I'm as real as you want me to be.*

Chapter Thirteen

A mother should never have to mourn the death of a son. Nor should a wife bear the loss of a husband taken from her much too soon. Angel Parkes had done both. She'd also gazed in the face of their killer who – in her mind – had gotten away with murder. Of course, the authorities didn't think so – calling it an unfortunate incident – offering their sympathies on one hand and telling Angel her husband and son were victims of a tragic accident. While the police officer that T-boned them had lived, both Angel's husband and son died. Over what? Expired plates! Instead of calling it in and having other officers be on the lookout for the car, the officer had pursued the vehicle, reaching excessive speeds through residential streets before finally blowing through a traffic light and ramming into Trenton's Prius at nearly a hundred miles per hour. Officer Pardy Ramirez returned to duty after six months, only to be killed in the line of duty several months after that.

While Angel should have felt remorse over the woman's death, in truth, she'd felt cheated that she didn't play a part in the woman's demise –

especially after Angel had gone to great lengths in planning Officer Ramirez's death. Since the policewoman had been so intent on stopping the car with expired tags, Angel was going to see that she got her wish. Only, when the woman approached her vehicle, Angel planned to be waiting with a surprise of her own. One shot fired point-blank from her husband's sawed-off shotgun. Sure, she might end up spending the rest of her life in prison, but it would be worth it to look into the eyes of the woman who destroyed her life as she pulled the trigger. It was the perfect retaliation, and Angel saw herself as the Avenging Angel – only she hadn't gotten her chance to avenge anything, and that was the catalyst that had set her on her current course.

Angel gripped the bottom of the storage shed, lifting the door up into the ceiling – her heart aching as the jet-black Mustang came into view. She stood looking at the car for several moments picturing her son, Andrew, staring out at her from behind the wheel. Angel shook off that vision as another appeared. She smiled, remembering her son's face when she'd gifted the car to him the day he received his driver's license.

Her husband, Trenton, was a sergeant in the Army, and they'd been stationed in Hawaii at the time. She'd pulled money out of savings and purchased the car without her husband's knowledge. Trenton was furious, but Angel had been able to soothe him over – at least until Andrew got his first speeding ticket on that same night. Trenton had threatened to take away his keys, but Andrew had insisted he hadn't meant to speed, claiming he was still getting used to the 'Stang's power. As usual, Angel had taken Andrew's side, and she and Trenton had gotten into yet another argument over their son. Angel sighed. There'd been too many arguments over Andrew, but there wouldn't be anymore.

Angel pulled the keys from her pocket and got inside the car. She closed her eyes, drinking in the smell. She hadn't dared to even pass a damp cloth over the dashboard for fear of removing even the tiniest of memories. The Mustang started on the first attempt, the sound of the engine bringing tears to her eyes. Andrew would have loved the way the rumble bounced off the inside of the steel cage. She pressed on the pedal and moved the horse out of its corral and into the light of day.

The horsey car – that was what Andrew called the muscle car when he was a little boy. They'd been stationed at Fort Leonard Wood, Missouri at the time, and the corporal living next door had a boss Mustang he liked to tinker on late at night, revving the engine, which would sometimes backfire. Not conducive for a sleeping child. After one such night when Andrew had been woken from sleep by the rumble of the engine, she'd gone into his room and told him it was just a car – assuring him there was nothing to cry about. The next day, she'd taken him next door and insisted the neighbor start the engine so her boy could associate the sound with the fear. Just as the engine rumbled to life, Andrew had keyed upon the emblem of the horse, pointing his tiny finger and proclaiming it to be a horsey car. The outing worked. Angel was thrilled when the next time he was woken by the sound – Andrew merely said, "The horsey car's awake" and went back to sleep without shedding a single tear.

She turned off the Mustang and went to her own car, backing it into the vacant space. She reached into her purse and removed the note she'd prepared, giving it a final read.

If you are reading this, my mission is done. I offer no apology, as I feel no regret for my actions – only the pride of a mother avenging the death of her son. And a wife exacting revenge for her husband's murder. I don't expect anyone to understand my reasoning, as I do not fully understand it myself. I've spent too many sleepless nights trying to find another solution; however, in my mind, this is the only way. I've spoken with my husband at length since his death, and he assures me I must execute the mission in its entirety if we are to be happy together in our afterlife. He visits me often, telling me this is the reason I was not with them that day, so that I would be alive to see justice served. I can't help but think I will not find peace until I myself am dead. I pray if you are reading this, that is the case. I should have been with them that day. It is only due to a minor argument with my husband that I refused to get in the car – a decision I've regretted for much too long. I will avenge their death so that they will welcome me when they see me again. There will be no arguing in the afterlife.

A bit rambling, but it'll have to do. Angel folded the note, then reached into the back seat and grabbed the duffle bag. Closing and locking the storage unit, she put both the bag and the note in the passenger seat of the Mustang, then pulled a cloth from the console and walked to the rear of the car. She stood staring at the license plate, wishing they'd never left the safety of the island. But they had when her husband received orders to the Fort Knox Army base in Kentucky. She knew the transfer to be a real possibility, but she'd hoped they would be able to stay in paradise a while longer. Everything changed after that transfer. She had no friends and Andrew hadn't weathered the adjustment very well. He'd become sullen and refused to do the simplest tasks. He hadn't even gotten around to changing out the plates when the accident occurred.

Accident – their deaths were no accident. They were murdered and someone needs to pay. Angel sucked in her breath and screamed into the air, not caring when her anguish bounced off the steel buildings that surrounded her. She gathered herself and wished for a moment she'd brought her meds. No, she needed a clear head – something she hadn't had in the last year.

Angel bent, spat onto the cloth, and ran it over the long-expired tags. Bait. A minor traffic infraction. Only this time, the officer would get more than they bargained for. Payback. Perfect. At least it would be if it were Ramirez.

Angel returned to the Mustang, slid behind the wheel, and closed the door. She unzipped the bag, pushed the guns aside, and removed a folder. She opened it and pulled out the Derby schedule, tracing a finger around the Balloon Glow slated to take place later this evening at the Kentucky fairgrounds. It was an evening demonstration of fiery light put on by the hot air balloons that were participating in the balloon race the following morning.

Andrew had always loved watching hot air balloons, which was the reason she'd chosen this particular day to begin avenging his death. She slipped the Derby schedule back into the folder and pulled out the map, unfolding it to see the marks she'd made. If she was able to exact her revenge and escape the city without being killed, she would move on to Cincinnati, Pittsburgh, and other major cities she'd circled. The only reasoning behind her choice of cities was that they needed to be large enough to have a high crime rate. If that were the case, police should be focusing on serious crimes, not minor infractions – if the cop was worrying about the small stuff, she felt they deserved to be punished. "I AM THE PUNISHER!"

Angel unfolded the note once more and signed the bottom before placing it and the map back inside the folder. She reached in the bag and brought out a framed photo of Trenton and Andrew standing next to the Mustang the day she'd given it to him. Good ole Trenton, smiling for the picture even though he was angry with her. He did that a lot – got angry with her and accused her of coddling their son. Maybe she did, but isn't that a mother's right? Trenton didn't have to worry about that anymore – she no longer had a son to coddle. At least not while she was alive.

Angel ran a finger across each of their images. "I'll be seeing you both soon. But not before I make things right."

***

The traffic heading into Louisville was beyond anything she'd imagined. Traffic on Dixie Highway was terrible, but from the time she entered the I-264, it was at a crawl. Unless an officer came up behind her, there was no way she would get lucky enough to be pulled over. Nor was she likely to get away after the stop.

Angel gripped the wheel when a pale green Prius moved up beside her. She looked again and realized it wasn't a Prius but a Chevy. *Hold it together, Angel. You've waited much too long for this.* Easing her grip, she went over her plan – take out as many female officers as she could before getting caught. She'd thought about taking out anyone with a badge but couldn't wrap her head around killing an innocent man. No, her victims must be women; that way, it would be easier to visualize Officer Ramirez when she pulled the trigger.

Chapter Fourteen

After nearly two weeks of shadowing Alex without picking up any new vibes, Jerry was beginning to think he'd gotten this one wrong. That, or it was still too early, as there were still plenty of events leading up to Derby Day. *Easy, Jerry, you know these things sometimes take time.*

Jerry placed his wallet in his right rear pocket. As he reached for his keys, his pinky brushed the bracelet Savannah insisted he carry, and a jolt surged through him. He picked up the bracelet and the feeling of dread intensified. *Today. Whatever is going to happen will be today.* He sat on the edge of the bed, closed his eyes, and intertwined the bracelet in his fingers. Immediately, an image of Alex flashed before his eyes then faded into a black horse. Jerry pushed his palms together in prayer form, watching behind closed eyelids as the horse turned into a rainbow of colors with wings. Jerry blew out a frustrated sigh. *What does it all mean?*

His cell rang, playing Seltzer's ringtone. Jerry opened his eyes and switched on the phone. "Seltzer?"

"McNeal, what the hell are you doing?"

"At the moment or in general?"

"I got an e-mail from the captain of the Louisville Police Department with a photo attached. Care to guess what that photo was of?"

"Shit!"

"Shit is right. The man's ready to adopt you."

"He'll change his mind when he meets me."

"You better make sure that doesn't happen. The e-mail said he wanted to thank me for sending one of my troopers down and wants to give the dog the key to the city. Said the dog is the talk of the town. Said everyone thinks he's one of theirs. What's that about anyhow?"

Jerry recognized the tone and knew what Seltzer was most upset about was that he himself had never got to see Gunter. Jerry looked at Gunter, who was currently lying on his back with his feet in the air. "Apparently, the dog thought his costume was funny."

"Funny, my ass; it's a damn public relations nightmare. Do you know what'll happen if Manning sees the picture? You'd better make sure there aren't any more photos. And damn sure not any with the two of you together. *Capiche*?"

"I understand."

"Yeah, you better make sure that dog understands. It's hard for me to cover your ass when you're on the front page of every newspaper."

"Roger that, sir."

"So, how's it going?" Seltzer's voice was calmer now. Jerry knew he'd just slipped into dad mode.

"It's going."

"Anything I can help with?"

"Not unless you're any good with puzzles."

"I take it you're not talking about jigsaw puzzles."

"No, sir."

"Ah, what the hell. Run it past me, and I'll give it a try."

"I know the who – she's a cop. And the when is today. I just don't know the what, other than I see horses."

"You're in Kentucky. You're supposed to see horses."

"That's the problem – they're everywhere, and I don't know what they mean."

"I thought you were there visiting your psychic friend. Can't you ask her?"

"I tried. The cop in question is her wife, and Savannah's not picking up anything."

"Is that normal?"

Jerry laughed. "Is anything in my life normal?"

"Maybe you need to find another friend."

Max. "You know, that's not a bad idea."

"Alright, I'll let you get to it. Remember to tell that dog to stay under the radar."

"Will do." Jerry clicked off the phone and dialed

Max's number.

"Hey, this is Max. If I'm not answering, I'm either at school or grounded from my phone. Leave a message and I'll call you back when the warden lets me out of lockdown."

Please don't let her be grounded. "Max, this is Jerry. I'm working on something here. I need you to concentrate on me and let me know if you get anything. I'm seeing a black horse along with the rainbow Pegasus. If you can, call me back today. It's pretty important."

Gunter opened his eyes and wagged his tail when Jerry pocketed the phone. "Yo, dog, the sergeant isn't happy with you."

The tail stilled and Gunter lowered his legs.

"He said you need to behave yourself, or your antics are going to get us both in trouble."

Gunter disappeared.

"Chicken!"

***

Savannah and Alex were in the kitchen when he went downstairs. Savannah turned when he came into the room, read his face, and dropped the glass she was holding. Recovering, she bent and started picking up the pieces.

Alex bent to help and Savannah waved her off. "I've got this."

Alex sat at the table and motioned for Jerry to do

the same. "You've got a pretty good poker face."

"So I've been told." *Too bad Savannah doesn't.*
"You okay?"

"You mean aside from knowing I might get killed today?"

Savannah looked up, her eyes blazing. "This is not a joking matter!"

"Sorry, babe. You know I'm not the crying type."

Savannah opened her mouth and Jerry raised his hand. She narrowed her eyes. "What? Are you going to lie to me and tell me everything's going to be okay?"

"No. I was going to tell you not to say something you might regret."

Savannah finished cleaning up the glass and left the room without another word.

Alex watched her go. "She's going to have a rough day."

"Not any worse than yours."

"That sounds encouraging."

"What I meant was – "

Alex laughed. "I know what you meant. I'm not going to dwell on things I have no control over. I have a twelve-hour shift starting at eleven. How do you want to play it?"

"Business as usual. With the exception of the bathroom, I go where you go. If I tell you to do something, don't stop to let it sink in, you do it. If I say duck, you duck. If I say drop – drop to the ground without questioning the reason."

"You still think I might get shot?"

"You got a vest?"

"Yes."

"Wear it."

***

Thousands of spectators milled about the fairgrounds, watching as balloon owners inflated balloons of all colors and shapes. Among the balloons were cats, an octopus, a pirate, a cactus, an owl, and even Humpy Dumpty had made an appearance. The balloon closest to them sent a roaring flame into the belly of the balloon and Jerry stiffened. *Easy, Jerry, it's just a balloon.*

Jerry felt something press against his leg and looked to see Gunter standing next to him. The weight of the dog's body pulled Jerry back from the brink. Jerry reached a hand to Gunter's head. *Thank you.*

"What are you thinking?"

She knows you're close to panicking. Jerry forced a smile. "I'm thinking I hate people."

Alex surveyed those standing near. "You hate crowds. There's a difference."

Alex was right – it was the crowd and the fact that so many people messed with his internal radar.

He had to resist following someone who set it off at every turn. Jerry pulled out his phone and looked at the screen. *Come on, Max, look at your phone.*

"It could be worse."

Jerry slipped the phone into his pocket. "How's that?"

"We could be on traffic duty."

"At least we'd be alone in the car."

Alex looked him in the eye. "Say we leave."

Okay. "You want to go?"

"No, hear me out. Say I were to call my supervisor right now and make up some story about being sick. Say he buys in to it and allows me to leave. Would that change things?"

Jerry closed his eyes and concentrated on her question. When he opened them, Alex was still staring at him. "It would change it for you."

"Meaning?"

"This person wants to kill cops."

Her eyes widened, then she recovered. "And we have a chance to stop it?"

Say no, Jerry, and you can both walk away. "Yes."

"Then we stay. Relax, McNeal – no, don't. Do whatever it is you do. Just don't have a panic attack and leave me out here on my own."

Shit. "Wouldn't think of it."

"Good to hear. How's your radar?"

"Going off like a pinball machine. Not just you."

Jerry waved his arms. "This. All of it."

"Want to take a walk?"

"I'm not leaving."

"With me."

"Lead the way." Jerry followed, eyes searching the crowd as Alex weaved in and around the spectators. The threat was here. He could feel it – it and hundreds of others that pleaded for his help. *Stay focused, Jerry.*

Alex turned and headed toward the main building. Once inside, she made her way toward the ladies' room, pausing just outside the door. "I've got this."

"Yell if there's trouble."

Alex's lip curled. "You'll be the first to know."

Actually, the second. Jerry gave Gunter a nod, relaxing slightly when the dog followed Alex into the room.

Jerry leaned against the wall and pulled out his cell phone. *Where are you, Max?* He started to put the phone away, but then searched through his phone book, found Max's mother's number, and breathed a sigh of relief when the woman answered.

"Hello? Mr. McNeal?"

"Mrs. Buchanan, I left Max a voice message and need her to check her phone."

"It will have to wait until tomorrow. Max is grounded for the rest of the day."

"Mrs. Buchanan, I respect that. Trust me. I

wouldn't ask if it weren't urgent."

"Urgent? Did Max do something wrong?"

"This has nothing to do with Max. But I think she can help me with a case I'm working on."

"A case? Max said you were finished with police work."

Jerry ran a hand over the back of his neck. "Please, Mrs. Buchanan, I'll explain everything later. Could you please just have Max check her messages?"

"Fine. Max! Mr. McNeal wants to talk to you."

"No, there's no time to explain everything. Just let Max listen to my message. She'll know what to do." Jerry switched off the phone to avoid further discussion. *What's taking Alex so long?* Jerry thought about opening the door to ask if she was alright, then remembered he'd sent Gunter in with her. *Relax, Jerry, don't draw unwanted attention. Just act normal.* Jerry pulled his phone from his pocket and pretended to look at the screen while scanning everyone in the lobby. He keyed on a man in a black t-shirt standing on the opposite side of the room. Thin with narrow-set eyes, Jerry knew he'd seen the man before. *Easy, Jerry, probably just a coincidence.*

Alex came out of the restroom, her hand under the arm of a woman. At that moment, every warning bell in Jerry's body went off. Instantly alert, Jerry looked for the man. The guy saw Jerry and turned, pretending to look at a poster on the wall. Jerry had been so focused on searching for a suspect, he hadn't noticed the print with two horses – one black and the other with wings – standing on their hindlegs rearing toward one another. *It's him. Easy, Jerry, don't scare him away.*

"Jerry, Angel here is not feeling well. I'm going to walk her to her car." Angel looked to be close to him in age and from her red-brimmed eyes, it was apparent she'd been crying.

Jerry felt like he was spinning out of control. He'd promised to stay with Alex, but if he followed her, the guy might see him as a threat and bolt. This was the guy. It had to be. His radar had nearly exploded when Alex came back into the room. "Go ahead. I'll be right behind you."

Alex's brows knitted together and Jerry forced a smile. Alex pulled up her chin and started for the door chatting to the woman as they walked. To Jerry's relief, Gunter stayed at Alex's side.

Jerry remained planted in place, pretended to make a call, then held the phone to his ear, all the while watching the man who had refocused his attention on Alex. Sure enough, the suspect tailed Alex and Angel as they made their way to the parking lot.

Jerry followed at a close distance. He felt the phone vibrate, glanced to see a message from Max, and pocketed it without reading it. *Too late, kiddo.*

Alex and the woman stopped at a black Mustang. The guy stayed back as Alex opened the door for the woman, helped her inside, and closed the door. As soon as Alex cleared the car, the man ducked out of view. Jerry was on him in an instant, pressing him against the hood of an SUV. Alex hurried to where they stood. "Is this the guy?"

"That or my radar needs a tune-up." The thing was, his radar should have stood down the second he grabbed the guy, but it was still soaring through his body, prickling as if every nerve ending was waking up.

"I just wanted to talk to you, Alex."

"Jeff?"

Jerry searched the man and pulled him from the hood. "You know this guy."

"Yes. We went to high school together. Jeff's a pacifist. I don't see him as being a killer."

Jeff's thin face paled. "A killer? Me? No, I just wanted to say hi and see how you're doing."

Jerry rolled his neck. The threat was here; he could feel it. He released Jeff. "Don't go anywhere."

The Mustang rumbled to life and Alex looked toward the car. "Shoot. I forgot to tell Angel her tags are expired. Hopefully, she can get them renewed before a cop pulls her over."

Jerry pulled his cell phone from his pocket. "I thought you were a cop."

Alex laughed a carefree laugh. "What can I say?

I'm a sucker for damsels in distress."

Jerry swiped the phone to bring up Max's message. "It's not a horse. It's a car. A car that looks like a horse."

A black horse. Hawaii. Rainbow. Pegasus. Wings – the woman's name is Angel. The images slammed together at once as Alex approached the driver's window of the Mustang, which had Hawaii plates with a rainbow stretched across the length of it. Jerry pulled his Glock from his waist. "ALEX, DROP!"

Gunter gripped Alex's arm, pulling her forward as the sound of a shotgun blast filled the air, the pellets peppering the Charger parked next to the Mustang.

As the Charger's windows shattered, Jerry watched Alex key her shoulder mike as she scrambled to the front of the car.

"You still there, Jeff?"

"I'm here."

"Good. Get behind that car and stay out of sight."

Jerry moved forward, keeping his Glock trained on Angel. As Alex made her way to the back of the Charger, Gunter appeared in the seat beside Angel. The woman screamed, opened the door, and fell out – backing away from Gunter. The dog had appeared wearing his K-9 uniform and followed Angel from the car, growling a menacing growl.

Alex took the lead, patting the woman down for

weapons and clamping restraints around her wrists. Alex glared at Angel as she told the dispatcher the suspect was in custody.

***

Jerry leaned against the hood of a police car, happy to be observing at a distance. Gunter sat at his side, both watching as Alex and another officer searched the Mustang. Alex handed a third officer a duffle bag then approached Jerry.

"There was a suicide note, which appeared to be death by cop. She was distraught at having lost both her husband and son." Alex wiped the sweat from her brow. "You were right: this was the beginning. Angel had a map showing all the cities she planned to hit after this one. There were a few newspaper articles about the deaths and another note telling of her plan to avenge their deaths. She even signed the suicide note Avenging Angel. Do you know why she tried to shoot me? Because I went back to tell her that her tags were expired."

"I guess some damsels don't like to be helped."

Alex bit at her bottom lip. "Thanks for being here."

"I almost blew it."

"Don't start that."

"Start what?"

"Playing the victim."

Sherry A. Burton

"Is that what I'm doing?"

"You and Savannah are good about beating yourselves up if things don't go the way you think they should. You have a gift. That doesn't make you infallible. Hell, even Superman had no power when kryptonite was involved."

"I'm no superhero."

"No, but you're my hero." Alex lifted her chin. "I'd kiss you on the cheek, but the reporters would take it out of context, and I'd have a hell of a time salvaging my rugged reputation."

"Shit."

"Problem?"

"I promised Seltzer I'd avoid the limelight."

"You go. I've got this."

"You sure?"

Alex winked. "They won't even know you were here. Hey, do me a favor."

"Name it."

"After you call for an Uber, can you give Savannah a call?"

"Chicken."

"Nope. Just don't want the boys here to see me cry." She turned without waiting for a reply.

Jerry pulled out his cell and typed a message to Max. > *You did good, kiddo. Your information saved the day. Tell your mom I said you're a hero.*

Jerry called for a ride then called Savannah.

"Jerry!? I was listening on the scanner. Is Alex

okay?"

Jerry could tell from her voice that she'd been crying. "Alex is fine. She said to tell you she will be home as soon as she can."

"Is it really over, Jerry?"

"Yes. Alex is safe."

"Aren't you going to tell me what happened?"

"Nope, this is Alex's story to tell." Jerry ended the call and looked at Gunter. "Well, we saved the girl again. You know, this hero thing is a pretty tough gig. At least in the movies, the hero always ends up with the girl."

Gunter placed his head under Jerry's hand as if to say *That's okay, you've got me.* Jerry knelt and scratched the K9's head. "You know, you're right. As consolation prizes go, you're not too bad."

*Join Jerry McNeal and his ghostly
K-9 partner as they put their gifts to good use in:*

Chosen Path
Book 4 in the Jerry McNeal series.

Available April 15, 2022 on Amazon Kindle:

https://www.amazon.com/gp/product/B09SFBH93
8

Please help me by leaving a review!

About the Author

Born in Kentucky, Sherry got her start in writing by pledging to write a happy ending to a good friend who was going through some really tough times. The story surprised her by taking over and practically writing itself. What started off as a way to make her friend smile started her on a journey that would forever change her life. Sherry readily admits to hearing voices and is convinced that being married to her best friend for forty-one-plus years goes a long way in helping her write happily-ever-afters.

Sherry resides in Michigan and spends most of her time writing from her home office, traveling to book signing events, and giving lectures on the Orphan Trains.